84762

84762

DATE DUE			
FEB 11 '87			
FEB 28 '87			
APR 18 '87			
JUN 1 '89			

"BOOKS MAY BE
RENEWED BY PHONE"

FORT MORGAN PUBLIC LIBRARY
414 MAIN STREET
FORT MORGAN, CO. 80701
867-9456

IVY LARKIN

ALSO BY MARY STOLZ

Night of Ghosts and Hermits:
Nocturnal Life on the Seashore

IVY LARKIN

A NOVEL BY

MARY STOLZ

HARCOURT BRACE JOVANOVICH, PUBLISHERS

SAN DIEGO   NEW YORK   LONDON

Library of Congress Cataloging-in-Publication Data

Stolz, Mary, 1920–
  Ivy Larkin.

  Summary: In New York City during the Depression, fourteen-year-old Ivy tries to cope with feelings of not belonging in her elegant private school and with her father's losing his job.
  [1. Family life—Fiction. 2. Depressions—1929—Fiction. 3. New York (City)—Fiction] I. Title.
PZ7.S87584Io 1986   [Fic]   86-4819
ISBN 0-15-239366-8

Designed by Julie Durrell

Printed in the United States of America

First edition

A B C D E

For Joan and Michael Carson, and for Tris,
from one of their loving aunts

PART ONE

ONE

WHERE WERE THE MOVING MEN? Why had they gone, leaving the Larkin furniture and the Larkin children abandoned on the sidewalk? Here were their boxes and barrels and beds, their rolled-up mattresses, their piles of books tied with twine, their bureaus and lamps, all of it spread out for everyone to see.

"Have you ever counted how many times we've moved?" Ivy Larkin demanded of her brother, who was sitting in an armchair looking disgusted.

"Nope. It'd make me mad and sad, counting up."

As usual, Pop had tried to make a song and dance of it.

"Off we're gonna shuffle," he'd sung, as they left the apartment up in Inwood this morning, "shuffle off to Buff—"

Ivy, at fourteen, had raced angrily past this kind of game playing several apartments ago. The two on upper Broadway; the three, no four, farther uptown in Inwood. Now they were trying to get into this place

3

on the Lower East Side, near the river, between the Brooklyn and Manhattan bridges.

But when would they get *inside*? They'd been here for hours, among their possessions, on the sidewalk. Why did their household belongings, which did not seem all that bad within walls, appear so frowsy and secondhand here on the sidewalk?

"It's like standing around undressed right in public," Ivy said to Francis, who was doing a cat's cradle and pretended not to hear.

From lowered lids, from the corners of her eyes, Ivy looked to see who was noticing. Nobody *seemed* to be, except some snotty, giggling little kids pushing each other around. That didn't fool her. All these people rushing or ambling past, detouring around them, muttering because they were taking up room—they were noticing, all right, feeling smug because *their* furniture was safe inside someplace. I don't think I'd even mind the moving part anymore, she thought miserably, if we could just get *inside*.

She shook her brother's shoulder. "Where are the moving men, Frank? Where are Pop and Mama?"

Frank did not look embarrassed. He looked pugnacious, ready to take somebody on. He was a year older than Ivy and a thousand years tougher.

"Frank, I asked you!"

"How should I know?"

Ivy turned her head from side to side, like a nervous animal. Look at them. Just *look* at them! Frank lolling back like a sultan. Megan, their six-year-old sister, in another chair, tidying Edward Bear's clothes with a little whisk broom, as unconcerned as if she were already home free.

Megan was any king's beautiful youngest daughter, but her looks had not proved insurance against her many unpredictable fears. The Larkins spent much of their time protecting her, but while they mounted guard in one place, terror would strike from another.

"All we can do," Pop and Mama said, "is see to it that she's never alone, never without at least one of us to—to make her understand that there's nothing to be afraid of."

So Megan was never alone, and never believed there was nothing to be afraid of. She's far from a dumb-bell, Ivy would think. She knows there's plenty to be afraid of, and not only strangers and the dark and elevators and cockroaches and radio programs like "The Shadow." And fairy tales.

Ivy liked to read aloud to her sister. One day, tired of Pooh (not *really* tired of him, just wanting a change), she'd switched to the Brothers Grimm. Megan had awakened that night and many nights afterward from screaming nightmares, and their parents hadn't much difficulty finding out the reason.

"But they're only stories!" Ivy had defended herself. "I thought she'd like them! For a change, only for a *change*."

"She's terrified by them, and you should have known she would be. Stepmothers stuffed in nail-lined barrels and rolled down hills. Talking horses' heads nailed to walls. Coffins everywhere! Gives me the shudders meself!" Pop had said.

"I didn't mean to frighten her!"

"Much good that does us now. Don't read to her, or stick to *Old Mother West Wind.*"

"You make us both sound stupid," Ivy had said stubbornly, and Pop had at once relented, pulling her close. "Sorry, Ivy, honey. Nobody's stupid, of course, and you meant no harm. But from this out—be careful."

Megan's fears. Who or what had caused them, why she had them, how long she'd have them—who knew the answer to any of that? Why should she be afraid of the dark when she had never found a thing in it to harm her? When was she even *in* the dark? A small lamp was on all night in the bedroom she and Megan shared, and the rest of the time it was day. Why be afraid of strangers when she'd known only kindness from them? Of cockroaches that after all couldn't *attack*, and fairy tales that after all were only stories? Why should she be so fearful of being alone when she had never been, even once in her life, by herself?

If I looked like her, Ivy told herself, I don't think anything would make me even slightly uneasy. I'd expect the world to part before me, like the Red Sea, and I would walk forward, looking neither left nor right, toward my goal.

What goal?

Megan seemed comfortable now, sitting back in Pop's Morris chair, readjusting Edward's clothes,

unaware of admiring glances garnered from passersby. ("*What* a little dolling," a woman said, stop-
ping in her tracks.)

"Where are the moving men?" Ivy asked her brother
again. "What are they going to do, leave us to *live*
out here? Where are Pop and Mama, will you tell
me?"

"They said they might walk over to Cherry Street
and tell Aunty and Unk we're here. Go look for them,
why don't you?"

"Well, I will."

"So go."

Ivy hesitated. "Don't leave Meggy." That got her a
patient glance. She wavered another moment, then
walked off, just not stamping.

The Lower East Side was nothing like Inwood. Here
life seemed to spill from apartment buildings onto
the streets. Radios blared out of windows, meshing
with the sounds of street traffic, river traffic. People
went loudly about their lives, everything out in the
open. And now came the bells of the Catholic church
Mama had made sure of, just a couple of blocks away.

Four o'clock! Would they never be indoors and safe?

Pushcart vendors lined the outside edge of the
sidewalks. At the curb an old droop-headed freckly
gray horse, hitched to an ice wagon, was feeding from
his canvas nosebag, tossing his head up and down to
get every morsel. He wore a straw hat, ears sticking
through a couple of holes, a red paper veteran's poppy
pinned to the brim. Wait'll Meggy sees him, thought

Ivy. Though she had not yet come to terms with any human beings except those in her family, Megan was passionate about animals.

Ivy walked on, calming a bit as she put distance between herself and the Larkin household junk. Pop called the stuff their lares and penates, but it still came out to mostly junk.

On brownstone stoops women and children sat talking, sewing, squabbling, staring. Some people had brought wooden kitchen chairs out to the sidewalk and sat there firmly, as if they were still indoors. Everywhere were children at street games. Hopscotch, statues, double dutch, stoop ball, jacks. They roller-skated riskily, bounced balls against the walls, played stickball in the street, defying traffic. They set up a tumult of laughter and screams and tears. They yelled at adults who yelled at them from windows and doorways.

There were a lot of men just hanging around, propped against the railings of areaways, talking lazily or irritably, smoking, spitting. They formed groups that clotted and dispersed and reformed.

The Larkin family went to the movies once a week, where the Pathé Newsreel never failed to show shots of what was called "The Army of the Unemployed." The voice behind the camera would be shrill, menacing. "They are selling apples! Seeking work! Sleeping in hallways, in subways, in ditches, in hobo heavens! They are hitting the road, riding the rods, always on the move. . . ."

Why, Ivy would wonder, does none of *this* frighten

8

Megan? It appeared not to. With the same glazed concentration she brought to Laurel and Hardy or Jeanette MacDonald, Megan gazed at the thin, sad men on the silver screen as they held out their apples, their little trays of shoelaces, to people who brushed angrily or coldly or shamefacedly past. She liked Tom Mix's horse and really came to attention for Rin-tin-tin. But Megan was not alarmed by jobless men with expressions furious or anxious or horribly blank as they looked into the cameras.

Why not? Or—why?

Should she be frightened by these strangers on the movie screen? They were, after all, mixed up with monkeys on bicycles and bathing beauties at Atlantic City. She was six years old. Her father had a job. She didn't know she was beautiful, didn't care that she was poor. She had her family, and that was that.

And here came her father and mother. Strolling! As if there was all the time in the world. As if they had not gone off and left their children alone in the middle of the furniture on the sidewalk with the moving men gone and no way to find out anything about anything. As if it didn't matter, any of it!

She started running toward them, yelling. Tears jerked down her cheeks. People *looked* at her. Shameful!

"Something wrong, Ivy?" her mother asked, sounding only mildly alarmed.

"Everything's *wrong!*" Ivy wiped her mouth and nose with the back of her hand. "You go off and nobody knows where and the moving men aren't anywhere and the furniture just sits there and sits there and people are staring at us and laughing—"

Her father pulled her head against his chest. "Calm down so," he said, patting her back. "There's nothing amiss atall. You're giving yourself the hard time over nothing."

Ivy felt her pulse begin to steady. She took a breath and said, sniffling, "Nothing, is it? We're the ones left behind with the moving men gone and the—"

"Stop now, Ivy, honey. The movers will be back when they've had their bite of lunch, and we just went around by way of letting your aunty know we are here and would not be displeased at the offer of a covered dish for our supper."

Mr. Larkin had a soft brogue he'd brought with him when he'd come to America from Ballyconneely, Ireland, as a lad with his mother and father. It broadened when he was anxious or angry or exhilarated, or sometimes, Ivy thought, just for the mischief in it, or when it was meant—as now—to *charm.* It did not charm everyone but never failed with his daughter Ivy.

And, indeed, the moving men had returned and were trundling stuff into the building on dollies, hoisting great loads on their backs. Ivy hated them. They loomed, with their beer bellies, their sweaty shirts, their mean expressions.

"What d'ya mean, *mean?*" Francis said when she pointed this out. "They're just doing their job and the stuff's heavy and they're hot. Why the he—heck are we moving in July, anyway? Usually it's October when we pull up stakes. That's a circus expression, did you know? Comes from when the circus is getting ready to— Hey, look. That one's coming to get the books. Think he'll say it?"

The man said it. "You people read all these?" he asked, eyeing the sixteen stacks of books in a disgruntled way. Every time, one of the movers said this. Never missed.

"We sure do," said Francis.

"Even little Miss America there?" the moving man asked but went off not waiting for an answer.

"Megan and Ivy," Mrs. Larkin said. "Come along with me. Your father and Francis can wait here while we get started in the apartment."

Ivy stood in the living room, looking around. It was sunny outdoors but dim in here. Bars at the windows, because of being on the first floor. Probably a good idea, but how awful it looked! Oh, God, she thought. How awful it all is! A hateful place they'd been brought to.

"Why are we here?" she asked her mother. "What are we *doing* here? We were perfectly all right where we were, and the sun came in in the morning, and I'll bet the sun never got in this place in its life. Why do we keep *doing* this?" she implored, but was obliged to fall silent as the moving men arrived with springs and mattresses and their parents' double headboard.

"That," said Mrs. Larkin, pointing to the head-board, "in the smaller bedroom. The cots in the larger one."

Sleepless I'll lie on my narrow cot, said Ivy to herself. From some poem she'd read? Had she made it up? *Sleepless I shall lie—*

"Mama, I asked you something. Why are we always moving? I hate this!"

Mrs. Larkin studied the upturned face for a moment and said, "There is something called a Depression going on—"

"I know that."

"Well, if you know that, you must also know that nobody has any money except rich people. We aren't rich people. Ivy, please. Let's get started emptying the boxes. This place is cheaper than where we were. Much cheaper. I'm sorry if you're unhappy, but there is nothing to be done about it, so you might as well stop—"

"You could let us go to a public school," Ivy interrupted. "That's one thing could be done about it."

Mrs. Larkin straightened, lifting her chin. Her body seemed to stiffen before she turned away and started untying the ropes that bound the big bureau. "I told those men to put this in our bedroom. People just don't do their jobs anymore. It's no wonder the whole world is going to pieces."

TWO

_____

IN INWOOD they'd gone to public school, an old yellow brick building with an entrance on one side for girls, on the other for boys, so that the lockers and rest rooms were separate. But classes were mixed. There'd been a cement yard in back with swings, basketball standards, and a roundabout. They'd walked to school from every apartment they'd lived in up there.

Even Megan had not minded going after the first tense and terrible attempts to get her to accept kindergarten. New situations, even a lot of old ones, told something awful on Megan's nerves. It puzzled her brother and sister, sometimes making them sad, sometimes fretful. But the teachers there, and the other children, had been more than kind (who was ever less than more than kind to Megan?), and she'd come to like school, though of course she would always prefer to be at home.

And now all, all was about to be changed, and they

were faced with a situation that this time had Ivy more alarmed than even Megan seemed to be. *Not* frightened, but furious. Resistant. Helpless.

"Nobody," she said aloud (she tended to do this when she was alone), "has any rights until they grow up. None at all!"

One Saturday in May, Mrs. Larkin on her day off from the hospital where she worked had taken her three children downtown on the Van Cortlandt subway to Forty-second Street, then across town on the shuttle, then uptown on the Lexington Avenue line, and then for a walk on a leafy street in the east sixties, nearly to Fifth Avenue.

During the entire trip, when questioned, she had just smiled and said, "You'll see."

They'd stopped in front of a five-story building that looked like a private mansion, which, once upon a time, it had been. Window boxes spilled over with petunias and geraniums. A brass plaque with small letters announced that this was The Holland School.

"Mama, what are we doing here?" Ivy demanded. "What is this place?"

Mrs. Larkin, with the air of proffering a surprise too delightful to be longer withheld, said, "*This* is The Holland School. I'll have you to know that it is one of the very ritziest private schools in New York."

"What's that got to do with us?"

"Well, today, you see, is kind of a—a game of chance," Mama said. "Nothing to lose, lots to gain, no harm done either way, see?"

"No," said Francis and Ivy together.

"It's like this. We have an appointment here with a man who's going to give you all some tests. You like taking tests. I mean, you're all so bright, which is one of the reasons I thought of this idea. After you've taken them . . ." She hesitated. "I mean, if it all works out, then you three might actually go to this school!"

"Why?" said Ivy.

"Yeah, why?" said Francis.

"How can you be so—so stubborn when I'm offering you a chance to— *Ohh!* Children are so *difficult!* This might be your chance to be lifted above the common herd—"

That's a funny thing for a person to say when she's always told us nobody is better than anybody else, Ivy thought.

As if seeing into her head, her mother went on. "That isn't what I mean, exactly. I mean this school could give you something that a public school just can't." She brushed her dark hair back impatiently and set her slender jaw. "The Holland School offers its students *innovative* teaching. Progressive ideas. Art, and music appreciation, and French and Latin and— something better than what you've been getting. You deserve something better."

You mean you do, Ivy thought.

Francis said, frowning, "You mean we'd have to ride three subways each way to get to *school?* That's crazy."

"Well, we haven't told you yet, but this summer

15

we're going to be moving. To a place where you'd
only have to ride the El to—"

"Moving!" Ivy shouted. "Mama! We moved last
October! How can we be moving again?"

"Can we go home now?" Megan asked.

Then their ordinarily cool and reserved mother began to cry, right out there on the sidewalk. Not loud.
Quiet tears fell down her face. "All right," she said.
"We'll go home. I should be used to—" She stopped,
cleared her throat, got a handkerchief from her purse,
and wiped her eyes. "Let's go."

Ivy and Francis looked at each other.

"No reason we shouldn't take the tests," Frank said.
"Long as we're here anyway."

Their mother was right about that. They enjoyed
tests of any kind. Not just the sort given in class-
rooms. "Spell *pneumonia,*" their father would say,
looking up from his book or his newspaper. "What's
7 x 84? What was Mark Twain's name, what was Sam
Weller's job, where did Pinocchio live? An archipel-
ago is a kind of saxaphone—true or false?" Any time,
any place. His children loved it. From time to time
he wrote out test papers, true and false lists, each
designed for the person taking it. Ivy's would be almost entirely about books. Francis got a mixture of
books, sports, and arithmetic. Megan was set puzzles
about animals—is a whale a fish or a mammal? Eeyore's favorite food is caviar—t or f? Where do grizzly
bears spend the Christmas holidays? Could you powder your nose with a puffin?

16

Tests were fun. They went into The Holland School to take some.

It was like somebody's private house. Somebody too rich to be real. The place seemed unreal to them. There was a great grandfather clock in the hall with gilded hands and a heavy brass pendulum moving back and forth very slowly, and a table with curvy legs. A green Buddha and a white china bowl filled with roses were on the table's pink marble top. A long mirror was behind it.

"Ah," said a gray-haired woman, entering from a room on the left, "Mrs. Larkin. Here you are. And these are—let me guess. Ivy, Francis, Megan, who are here to look us over. Come into my office, won't you?" she said, as if asking a favor.

"Are you Mrs. Stebbins?" Mama asked.

"Indeed I am. Do come."

The office, with a rug that Ivy supposed was Persian on the dark polished floor and a desk that also had a bowl of roses on it, looked to the children like a room in a moving picture. Sunlight fell softly on leather chairs, on walls of books. There was a fireplace with a pleated gold paper fan in it and pictures of birds on the wall.

The three of them sat unspeaking, side by side on a sofa, while Mrs. Stebbins explained that the psychologist who would be giving them the tests was upstairs awaiting them. That was what she said. "Awaiting."

Later, when Ivy thought about it, she could never get the day properly straightened out. How long they sat while their mother talked with Mrs. Stebbins, like people at a tea party with no tea. The climb up to a large, well-lit room on the fourth floor. ("We have an elevator, but our boys and girls are not encouraged to use it as walking up stairs is good for young limbs.") The psychologist, a man named something or other, talked to them for a long time after inviting Mama to go back downstairs with Mrs. Stebbins.

At last he gave them each a set of printed questions and diagrams along with a blue booklet to put the answers in, and told them they could start when they wished, there was no hurry.

The day was a blur—except for an unforgettable glimpse of some Holland students passing the room, all well dressed, carelessly self-assured, laughing and talking, moving about as if they owned the place.

As if they were on Parnassus, thought Ivy, who had read a lot of Bulfinch. They all, every single one of them, seemed to be tall.

The tests, of course, were fun.

If I'd understood what was actually happening, what we were being committed to, she thought a few weeks later, I'd have answered everything wrong. I'd have misbehaved something awful. Brought gum to chew and stuck it under the desk so that man could see me do it. Used bad language to Mrs. Stebbins. I'd have told them their school didn't look like a school or feel like a school and I didn't want any part of it.

She told herself this when, a month later, a letter came informing Mr. and Mrs. Larkin that The Holland School would be delighted to accept all three children on full scholarship.

She'd done none of those things, and would not have, even had she known that her fate was being decided in that sunny room as she wrote in the blue book, forgetful of anything but the challenge of a set of questions to which she knew most of the answers because she had parents who answered questions and bought books and thought that learning was fun. ("Always carry a book," their father had instructed them, "in case the subway stops.")

She could not fail her mother, though she considered that her mother had failed her.

Ivy yearned to be grown up. When you were a child, you did what they wanted. Willy-nilly. Helter-skelter. Pell and mell. You were hocussed and pocussed from one place to another with no say about it at all. You could have friends where you were, like the school you were going to, the apartment you lived in where you and your sister had a bedroom together and Francis one of his own. You could lose all that when *they* decided you would.

On the first night in the new apartment, Ivy, refusing to read, lay on her cot and looked resentfully over at Francis, who was either reading the funnies or pretending to.

The three of them were jammed together in what Mama called the "larger bedroom," Francis against one wall, Megan in the middle, Ivy at the other wall. Between the beds, orange crates were disguised as tables. The bureau with three big drawers. A chair. That was it, their room. Not even curtains yet, just blinds pulled down in front of the barred windows, to hide her and her brother and sister from people going past in the courtyard.

"It's like being in jail," she said to the ceiling.

Megan glanced over uneasily.

"I hate it!"

"Hate what?" Megan asked.

"Everything! All of it!"

Finding this too much to grapple with, Megan resumed reading aloud to Edward from *Now We Are Six*.

"Hey, listen to this," said Francis. "In the first one, Krazy Kat is writing on a long sheet of paper, and Ignatz Mouse is saying, 'That's a queer letter you're writing to yourself today,' and Krazy says, 'Yes, it's a Chinese letta,' and Ignatz says, 'I didn't know you could write in Chinese,' and Krazy, who's smoking a cigar now, says, 'Sure, I can't,' and in the next one Ignatz says—"

"Frank, will you *shut up?*"

"Don't you want to hear the end?"

"You know why we're here, don't you? Not to be closer to Aunty and Unk, the way she says. I don't even think it's all that much cheaper. We're here because that school is going to be expensive. Scholarships, baloney. I heard Pop saying about extra costs and hidden costs and costs that he says scare him. Pop's scared, and we don't want to go there, and it's all because she wants to be—lah-di-dah or something. Except that we're the ones will be lah-di-dahing for her up in that school for snobs."

"They can't *all* be snobs," Frank said uncertainly.

"Frank! I own two skirts, one dress, three blouses, two sweaters, two pairs of shoes, and a four-year-old coat that Geraldine wore out before she gave it to me."

"What's that got to do with the price of peanuts?"

"Oh, God!"

"You're just talking about clothes. I don't care about clothes."

"Well, let me tell you, Francis Larkin, you may have a chance to change your mind. When you have to wear that old jacket that the sleeves are too short on and your pants that can't be let down anymore, you may just begin to care about clothes when you look around you up there."

"Well, that's one worry you don't have, huh? I bet you haven't grown an inch in two years."

Ivy jerked, as if struck. "You don't have to make fun of me, Frank," she said shakily. "That's something you don't have to do."

"Hey, I wasn't making fun, Ivy. I was only saying— Hey, I'm sorry."

"Oh, skip it." She turned on her side, pulling the sheet up to her ears, though it was hot and airless in their room.

21

"Ah, come on, Ivy," he said. "Anyway, we don't have to worry about that school yet. We've got the whole summer ahead of us. Anyway, practically."

Megan, at that, sang out in tones of perfect joy, "We'll be going to the farm soon! Pretty soon we'll be going to the farm!"

It was true, it was true. Before whatever that school might bring, there was this much certain happiness—their two weeks on Aunt Anna's farm.

PART TWO

THREE

——————

Each summer they spent two weeks on their Uncle Jim's farm in upstate New York. He was the husband of one of Mrs. Larkin's sisters. There were three of them. Aunty—Aunt Kate—who lived on Cherry Street. Aunt Tess, who was backward and lived with Uncle Jim and Aunt Anna on the farm. And Aunt Anna—bountiful, beautiful, generous, loving, lovely tempered, welcoming Aunt Anna, who gathered them each time in her plump enfolding arms and made them feel wanted, despite their cousin Geraldine's candid displeasure and Aunt Tess's uneasy grumbling. Despite the extra work it made for her, who already toiled from dawn to dark, as Geraldine (who did not noticeably toil) frequently pointed out to Ivy.

The farm was at once the most substantial and most dreamlike sphere they knew. Every creature, every structure, every sweep of meadow and rise of hill, every path and tree and bush and butterfly existed in their minds, unchanged and longed for, during fifty weeks of exile.

To pick real fruit—plums, peaches, cherries, currants, raspberries, blackberries—from real trees and bushes was, to the Larkin children, an act miraculous, miraculous as the multiplying of loaves and fishes, the changing of the water into wine at the wedding at Cana, the burning of the bush that was not consumed. To see birds, not pigeons or sparrows, but thrushes and thrashers and indigo buntings; to watch cows trot barnward, great udders swinging, and to see them milked; to hear a rooster boast at the top of his voice about the day he was bringing into being—all this, though it had ceased to astonish, continued to awe them.

Ivy, though she had been there every summer since she could remember, never believed, when leaving, that she would see the farm again. A year would have to pass before once again they rushed off the Greyhound bus to find Uncle Jim waiting for them as he always did. An entire year! Any fool knew that the only year that passed was the one you'd left behind you. Fifty weeks stretching ahead was impassable. She would leave the farm in a state of pain and misery only possible to conceal because Geraldine had once said that if it made her so unhappy to leave, probably it would be better if she didn't come in the first place.

But now—oh, now they were arriving, and two weeks lay before them like a land of dreams.

The Greyhound bus pulled up with a shriek of brakes at the curb in front of Paulson's Drug Store, and the Larkin children, well mannered, allowed the grownups to get off first. Then, hearts thumping, they leaped to the sidewalk, where Uncle Jim was waiting.

Thinning hair, bushy mustache, gleaming specs. Oh, you are so beautiful, Ivy thought. You are such a beautiful *man*.

"Here you are," he said, as if with satisfaction. He shook hands with Francis, hugged Ivy, and swept Megan up in his arms. "Truck's right down the street."

Frank picked up the Navy duffle bag that Pop had carried as a sailor in the World War, that now held all their clothes for two weeks, and he and Ivy walked behind their uncle, unspeaking. I know what he's feeling, Ivy told herself. Just what I am. That it's too wonderful for words. She looked around hungrily at the street of this town with the hallowed name, Glens Falls. It hadn't changed. Nothing had changed! And there was the Model-T Ford truck, and it hadn't changed either!

Dizzy with joy, she stumbled, and Uncle Jim, looking over his shoulder, said "Whoops adaisy!"—making her eyes mist over.

Megan sat in the cab beside her uncle. Edward Bear, in overalls, sat on her lap. But Frank and Ivy rode in back, holding onto the stock boards, gazing with famished eyes at passing farms and fields, waiting for the turn in the road and the moment they'd been yearning for all these weeks and months.

After miles of paved roads, with horses and cattle

27

grazing in fields on either side, and Burma Shave signs (*If you don't know whose signs these are, you haven't traveled very far*) and barns and farms and an occasional roadhouse offering EATS, they turned onto a dirt road. Ivy and Francis exchanged a quick glance and drew themselves up in a condition of bliss so acute they found it hard to breathe.

There!!!

They rounded a curve and all was revealed to them. Lazing under the August sun were the big barn, the outbuildings, the white clapboard house, just as they had left it all last year. And Aunt Anna, in an apron, standing on the veranda (oh, what a grand word, *veranda!*) with Ranger, the collie, beside her, and no sign of Geraldine.

The white, three-story house with striped blue awnings and an *attic* was just the same. There were the same flowers growing beside the driveway and in beds alongside the house. Behind the house, unseen but *there*, was the garden where grew rows of lettuce and beans and peas and tomatoes and corn, and netted beds of berries and currants. Beyond that, climbing a low hill, was the orchard of peaches and apples and cherries. Cows stood or lolled in a meadow where daisies and buttercups and Queen Anne's lace were growing.

> *Queen Anne, Queen Anne is dead and gone*
> *(She died a summer's day),*
> *But left her lace to whiten on*
> *Each weed-entangled way!*

Oh, the weed-entangled ways and days that lay before them now! And it was all—*all*—more wonderful even than it had been in those year-long dreams. The air was fresher, sweeter, hotter, grassier, more crowded with bees and butterflies and singing birds.

And Aunt Anna, who always smelled of gingersnaps, was fatter and dearer than ever.

"Well," she said, opening her arms wide. "Here are my three city mice, and I'm so glad to see you!"

Francis and Megan hurled themselves at her. But Ivy, threatened with joy, as if she were casting sparks, began to run. She tore up to the orchard, down along the fenced meadow, back to the barn. There the dusk, shot with shifting sunbeams and a hot, strawy smell, drew her helplessly in.

She walked slowly, shaken with reverence, gazing up at old dark beams with shining adz marks made by strong hands now long at rest. She noted how the sun came through the great doors and lay like a gold-specked carpet on the wide board floors. She touched each stanchion on the long cement apron, where, come evening, the cows would stand to be milked, swishing their tails, turning their mild-eyed heads around for a look at the milker. She stood for minutes looking into the horse stall. Violet, the big mare, did not use it in summer, but her horsey fragrance lingered. Tack hung on nails outside the stall, and inside a few oats were scattered on the swept floor. Uncle Jim's barn was bigger than the house and just as clean. Knowing she should go back and try to explain her

flight to Aunt Anna, Ivy looked at the ladder leading
to the hayloft and began to climb.

In a far corner, in a shadowed place near a slatted
window where sunlight now came through in a dusty
ray, was an old bearskin. The head, yellow teeth
bared, was supposed to be snarling, but Ivy found its
expression sad. It had rough, shabby fur and a rank
odor, and its big paws with enormous curved brown
claws lay on the loft floor in a lamed attitude. Ivy's
mother, who did not want any animal hunted, hated
this bear. ("Anna, how can you stand having that
terrible thing up there? Why don't you get *rid* of it?"
"Well, Moira, after all, it's been there so long. And
we didn't shoot it, Jim or I. His father did. And what
would I do with it? Can't give it away. Who'd want
it? Stay out of the barn if it bothers you.")
Ivy adored the bear. She lay down on him now, as
she had in summers past, and said, "Here I am, old
thing. I told you I'd be back." She patted the heavy
head, then put her arms around it and leaned over
to gaze into his dull glass eye. He had only one. "I
missed you," she whispered. In a little while she got
to her feet, feeling that now she'd be able to talk to
people without choking up or crying.

"Boy," said Francis when she came into the house
by the front door. "You could walk under a snake's
belly with stilts on. Don't you have any manners at
all?"
Choking up after all and ready to burst into tears,

Ivy put her head down and brushed past him to the kitchen, redolent of a kind of cooking they never knew at home.

"Aunt Anna! Aunt Anna! I didn't mean not to have any manners! I was so happy to be here that I just had to—I had to *run*. I couldn't help it!"

"That's all right, dearie," said her aunt, rolling out a piecrust on a floury board. "It doesn't matter."

Ivy found that hurtful. Aunt Anna sounded as if it really didn't matter what she did. She did not offer to hug Ivy, as she had Megan and Francis. Of course, now her hands were covered with flour. Probably— certainly—the moment for that kind of greeting was past.

Sighing for her blunders, Ivy looked around the kitchen and made another.

They had done it again! During the winter, while her back was turned, they had made more *improvements! Changed* things.

Two years ago, she'd come up to find the farm electrified. Gone were the kerosene lamps with their lovely flowered bases and shades that had made evenings here so softly mysterious, so not like everything harsh in the city. Those lamps, the light of them, glowed in her memory all year, an evening radiance entwined with evening sounds—cows mooing in the meadow as darkness came, the song of crickets, the creak of the porch swing, the shuffling of huge moths against the screens. Gone had been the brass candlesticks, like plates with handles, that they had used to light their way to bed. Electric light switches everywhere! Ivy had cried out in unthinking protest then, and did so now, seeing that one of the glories of the farm kitchen was gone. Since she had first been coming here, the pump at the kitchen sink had enraptured her. An iron pump with a long curving handle that a person moved up and down to get water gushing into the tin sink. There was another much larger pump over the well behind the house.

"Is the outside one gone, too?" she asked her aunt in a shrill voice.

"What one gone, too? I don't know what you mean, Ivy."

"The pump! The pumps! Where did the pump at the sink go?"

"Oh, my. You do tend to be romantic about inconveniences," said Aunt Anna, laughing.

"Romantic," said Geraldine, gliding into the kitchen. "That's what you call it, Ma? Selfish is more like it. Come along, Ivy, and let me show you some more of our *un*sentimental conveniences. Come *on*." She went toward what had been the summer kitchen.

"Geraldine," said her mother. "Remember that Ivy is our guest.

"Don't I know it."

"Gerry!"

"Okay, okay. Come along, little guest, Ivy. Let me show you."

Ivy glanced imploringly at her aunt, who turned out her hands, leaving it to her whether to stay or to follow her cousin. She followed. She would have tagged after Geraldine all the time, if permitted. She was not permitted. Geraldine ignored her, now and then snapped at her, occasionally was really sweet. Aunt Anna said her daughter was moody. Francis, who didn't care one way or the other, said she was a stuck-up dope. Megan liked her, and naturally Geraldine liked Megan. Beauties, both of them, but unlike Megan, Geraldine was perfectly aware of how she looked.

This family, Ivy would say to herself, does produce gorgeous *tall* people. Meggy and Geraldine. Aunt Kate. Frank was as handsome as he could be without making himself ridiculous. A combination of his parents, with his father's face and build, his mother's dark, shining hair. We also, she'd add, angrily or sadly according to the day, produce the likes of me. Ugly— no, *plain*—ducklings.

"Are you coming or aren't you?" Geraldine said.

Ivy came to attention. "Yes." She followed Gerry into a bathroom. Bathroom! With a toilet and a tub and a sink and a linoleum floor. This room had been the screened summer kitchen, where Aunt Anna did her laundry. There had been two big soapstone sinks with a wringer between them, and an ironing board always set up and a stove on which to heat the flat-irons that Aunt Anna used alternately, working with one while the other grew hot. She was a beautiful ironer. The tiniest ruffles bloomed at her touch. There had been an extra icebox in here, and a cider press and an ice-cream freezer and a churn for butter and—

"Where's the summer kitchen?" she demanded of Geraldine. "What happened to it?"

33

Geraldine flung her lovely arms upward. "Poof! In a cloud of smoke!"

"But where does—how does Aunt Anna do her laundry?"

"*Her* laundry? Surely you mean the family's laundry? Yours, too, of course, now that *you* three are here. The tubs are in the cellar now. And Ma has an electric iron. She irons in the kitchen with an electric iron. Isn't that spiffy? And we can all take a bath whenever we want, without having to boil water on the stove and fill that old galvanized tub and empty that old galvanized tub, and it's all too horribly modern, isn't it, Ivy?"

"I think it's nice for you," Ivy said miserably.

"Mmm. I'll bet. Whoops, there's Harry." She ran out of the bathroom, through the kitchen. "Bye, Ma. I'll be back."

"When?"

"Harry and I are going for a spin, that's all. Bye. Oh, hi, Meggy. See you in a bit." The screen door banged and she was gone.

Ivy, at the window, watched her get into an old flivver parked in the drive. Geraldine's boyfriend. One of them. She always had boys hanging around, but it was only last year she'd started calling them boyfriends.

In the kitchen, Megan was sitting next to the big black coal range with a young cat on her lap, Edward on the floor beside her.

"Lookit, Ivy," she said, holding up the silver striped

tabby. "His name is Mousetrap. Mousetrap," she murmured, cuddling the cat next to her cheek. He took it patiently. "Isn't he lovely?"

Ivy knelt and patted the small silky head, so different from the bear's shaggy skull, and said, "He's adorable." What an awful name, she thought, but did not say.

Looking up, she caught her aunt gazing at Megan lovingly, shaking her head as if at some marvel. Megan didn't have to say or do anything in particular to affect people that way. All she had to do was *be* to cause expressions to change from everyday aspects to tenderness, to doting, to loving. Mostly, she affected her sister the same way.

Except. But.

Ivy read a lot of poetry. There was a young poet, Edna St. Vincent Millay, who lived not far from where the Larkins now did, in New York City. Miss Millay had written a verse that ended:

Oh fishermen and farmers may see me and forget,
But I'll be a bitter berry in your brewing yet.

Ivy often thought of those lines. Not that she would be or would ever want to be a bitter berry in Megan's cup of life. It was more the other way around. And not that Megan would *ever* want to be a bitter berry in anybody's brewing. She just, Ivy thought with what she hoped was resignation, isn't going to be able to help it.

Megan and Geraldine. People couldn't look like that and not make other people, some of the time, bitter.

A silent sickness welled in Ivy sometimes when she thought about Megan, whom she loved and hated. No, no, no . . . *not* hated. Never. Was jealous of. No, envious of. Envy: discontent at the sight of another's excellence or good fortune. Jealousy and envy were awful words, horrible words. Megan's fortune was not completely good. Born beautiful but scared. She couldn't help that. People said she'd outgrow it. She can't help looking the way she does, either, Ivy would remind herself. She wasn't going to grow out of that. Probably just get more so. Baby swans didn't grow up to be ugly ducks.

Did plain ducklings ever grow up to be swans? Ivy didn't think so.

FOUR

Something had happened to Aunt Tess when she was born that had hurt her brain, so that people who didn't understand or were unkind called her feeble-minded. She was not. Her speech was difficult to understand, and she could not get a job or live by herself, but she was a big help to Aunt Anna around the house, and a help to Uncle Jim, too, since she loved to milk the cows and did it very well. She was strong and could carry the carpets out to the line and whack away at them with a rattan beater until there wasn't a speck of dust left. She tatted lots of things.

Aunt Tess had lived with Aunt Anna and Uncle Jim since their marriage, and if she had not done so, she would have had to be in a mental home.

Megan loved Aunt Tess. Francis was patient with her and, of the three Larkin children, was the only one who really understood what she was saying and could answer her right away. Ivy, though she tried to conceal it, did not like her. She picked up only about one word in ten when Aunt Tess spoke, and Aunt Tess tended to lose her temper under those conditions. Most painful of all to Ivy, she was the only McManus sister who was short, about an inch taller than Ivy. In a family of tall people—the sisters had all married men over six feet—Ivy and her Aunt Tess looked lopped off. Megan, at six, was already nearly Ivy's height. Francis gangled up like a stork.

Me and Aunt Tess, Ivy would think in despair. Aunt Tess and me. That was the bitter berry in *her* summer brew.

This year she was determined to put odious comparisons out of mind. If she succeeded at that, surely she'd be able to get along with Aunt Tess as well as everybody else. Success here would make her aunt and uncle like her better. Not Geraldine, whom she admired too much and would have given anything to be like or to be friends with, anyway. Not a chance of either, ever. But the others . . . surely this year she would manage to be better liked by her upstate relatives upon whom, it sometimes seemed to her, her only happiness depended.

Now, on the first day, Aunt Tess came into the kitchen, stumbling a little, smiling. She smiled unless she was angry. She had small eyes and dust-colored hair.

"Frwank," she said thickly.

Frank, thought Ivy. That's plain enough. She's talking about Frank.

A long sentence followed. Here and there Ivy seized

a word. *Today* was one. *Happy,* another. Please? Peas? *Trees?*

"Of course we're happy to have them," Aunt Anna said. She filled the fluted piecrust with fresh sliced peaches that she'd sprinkled with flour, sugar, cinnamon, salt, lemon juice, and grated rind. She dotted bits of butter over the surface, deftly fitted on the top crust. "It's all right if he climbs trees, Tess. He's a big boy. Megan and Ivy are here, too, of course," she pointed out.

Still holding Mousetrap, Megan jumped up and put out her hand. Aunt Tess never kissed anybody. She shook hands. Now she pumped Megan's up and down vigorously and turned away.

"Ivy," said Aunt Anna in a low voice, "please offer your hand. She doesn't mean to be rude. She simply is, sometimes."

But when Ivy rushed around and pushed her hand forward, Aunt Tess kept her arms down and scowled. "Pest!" she said, and stumped off. Clear as anything. Pest.

"Dearie," said Aunt Anna, "don't hold it against her. She takes notions. Nobody knows why. Actually, she's very fond of you, I happen to know."

I happen to know she's not fond of me, and I can't stand her, Ivy thought. She said, "I understand, Aunt Anna. I do try."

"Of course you do. Why don't you go up and unpack your duffel bag?" She frowned slightly. "I had thought of putting a cot in Tess's room for you—"

Ivy's heart at once turned to stone and seemed to plummet in her chest. She stood rigidly, waiting.

"But it won't do, I'm afraid. She seems upset."

Breathe again.

"I guess you and Frank can stay another year in the sewing room," said her aunt. "I hope you undress in privacy, both of you."

Ivy, who paid little attention to privacy with her brother and sister, said, "Well, sure." If that was what Aunt Anna wanted—

"That's settled then. You haven't said what you think of my lovely bathroom."

"It's wonderful for you."

And of course it was wonderful for the family to have an inside bathroom and electricity and taps over the sink instead of the beautiful old pump. She supposed the outhouse was gone, too. She hadn't thought to look when she'd been running about like a wild rabbit. But why would they keep it, now that there was a bathroom right in the house where the summer kitchen had been? The outhouse, a little wooden structure with a small half-moon cut in the door and a small red hand that you put up when you went in, so no one else would, had had a strong smell. Ivy had never minded. It was part of the farm. Sitting in there on a hole in a wooden board, with the warning hand up, you could leaf through a Montgomery Ward catalog that hung on a nail, or peek through chinks at the people coming and going or at the cows cropping clover and timothy in the meadow.

She walked to the kitchen window and looked out. Yup. Gone, the path to it grassed over.

They're ruining my farm with their improvements, she said to herself with deep and painful resentment, and recognized her own selfishness. There was a man named Dr. Coué, who kept telling the American people that the way to be happy and stop the Depression was for everybody to say, every day, out loud, "Day by day in every way I'm getting better and better." Pop thought Dr. Coué was pretty funny.

Day by day, in every way, Ivy said to herself now, I'm getting brattier and brattier.

After supper, Aunt Anna said, "Ivy, you and Gerry clear the table, please. The rest of you, scoot."

Ivy glanced at her cousin, but Geraldine was already stacking plates, humming under her breath. Aunt Tess could not be asked to help with the dishes because she was apt to drop them. Megan was too young, and Uncle Jim too tired from his long day's farm work to help in the kitchen. But Ivy could not see why Francis was always allowed—told—to scoot.

She composed in her mind sentences to suggest to Aunt Anna that her brother could take his turn, not just with the dishes, but helping to prepare vegetables and stuff like that that she and Geraldine were always asked to do. She wouldn't use the sentences, being already off on the wrong foot. At home, Frank was asked to help, but he had a way of not being around when the time came, or of having homework, a stomachache, something or other that would allow him to escape "woman's work." Mama never insisted, so long as he did his share of "man's work," which seemed to Ivy to consist of nailing picture hooks in the wall or changing a washer in a tap.

It did not seem to her that the scales of life were evenly balanced between girls and boys, men and women. It did not seem, either, that there was anything to be done about it.

Aunt Anna washed the dishes in a soapy basin, rinsed in a clear one, stacked on the wooden drainboard faster than Geraldine could dry. Ivy, who knew where everything went, put away.

"Ivy-wivy here doesn't approve of our improvements," Geraldine commented, holding up a glass for inspection and handing it back to her mother. "Did you know that, Ma? She longs for old discomforts. Ours, not her own."

"That's not so!" Ivy said. "I think it's wonderful for you, all of it. I only . . . only—" She broke off, defeated.

"I've had quite enough of this," Aunt Anna said. "I can understand what Ivy's feeling. She's *fanciful* about the farm. Nostalgic. Dear me, I still get to longing for Father's old horse and buggy sometimes. Ivy doesn't understand about actually living here, especially in winter." She looked at her niece with a smile. "You try floundering through snow up to your hips to get to that outhouse on a January night and see if a bathroom right in the house doesn't seem like heaven on earth."

Ivy, who would have sold her birthright (though if she had one, she could not imagine what it could be) to be up to her hips in snow on the farm, to see it and be here in the winter, said only, "I think it's wonderful for you."

"You're a broken record," said Geraldine. "We could put you on the Victrola and let you go round and round."

"Geraldine! Will you stop that this *instant!*" said her mother. "Sometimes you have the manners of a turkey gobbler."

Geraldine flushed, glared at Ivy, and fell silent through the rest of the washing-up.

Then, surprisingly, she elected to sit on the veranda with the rest of the family as evening came on. There were several wicker chairs and rockers here, and a wooden porch swing, big enough for two, suspended on chains from a ceiling beam. Aunt Tess and Megan sat there, Aunt Tess pushing gently with the tips of her toes. The chains creaked, crickets rasped in the grass, the sweet clink-clunk of a cowbell sounded in the darkling meadow. Birds twittered a little, stirring the bushes, and grew silent. A mild wind fingered the treetops and sang from pole to pole in the telephone wires. Fireflies flicked here, there, near, far. You could never fix on one firefly. You had to widen your eyes to take in an impression of all of them, glinting on and off.

Now the moon rose, looking like a banana, so yellow and plump and low in the sky.

43

Ivy, sitting on the steps with her back to the rest of them, was so acutely aware of it all that tears filled her eyes and fell on her skinny knees. In the gloaming, none of them noticed that.

FIVE

OF THE LARKIN CHILDREN, only Francis had been named for a saint. Mr. Larkin had named Ivy after a story by an Irish writer. He said it was the best short story he'd ever read, "Ivy Day in the Committee Room." Ivy, when she was old enough, had tried to read it. She was going to try again in maybe thirty years. Megan had been named for Pop's mother, so she'd been lucky in this as in so much else.

Ivy was an awful name, and difficult to forgive. At her confirmation, she'd taken the name of Blaise, for the patron saint of throats. Pop said it was also the name of a famous Catholic philosopher and mathematician. Ivy only knew that Blaise Larkin was a name she could live with happily. She tried to get the others to call her that but didn't expect to succeed and didn't. Never mind. When she was grown and on her own, she would be Blaise Larkin. She planned to be a librarian, to spend her life surrounded by books.

The story in the family was that no one had taught her how to read. She'd simply picked up one of those linen books of her babyhood and after days of scrutiny had settled beside her brother and started reading aloud: " 'There was an old woman who lived in a shoe . . .' "

Here on the farm, she read trash, pulp magazines bought by Geraldine, Street and Smith love stories, stacked head-high in a corner of the barn loft. Ivy was glad her cousin didn't throw them out, though she saw no reason for keeping them. Nobody would want to reread a Street and Smith love story. How could you even tell if you were rereading one?

Now, lying on her brown bear (of course he was *her* brown bear since nobody else wanted or cared for him) on a rainy afternoon a few days after they'd arrived at the farm, her head against the bear's head, the future Blaise Larkin, librarian, worked her way contentedly through a pile of pulps. An afternoon's such reading left her feeling stuffed, as if she'd been gorging on candy.

She dropped the issue she'd been reading onto a pile of those she'd finished and said aloud, "This is dumb!"

To yearn all year for the farm, and then, when she got here, climb up to a hayloft to read Geraldine's rubbish.

Still, it was too wet to run around the fields following Uncle Jim, hoping for a ride on the tractor, or to climb trees or splash in the shallow pond by the icehouse or lie in the orchard dreaming.

She gazed at the peaked, beamed ceiling. Rain tin-tinnabulated on the tin roof, raked past the open loft door. She pictured towns and cities, fields and farms and forests under the falling rain. Walking to the loft door, she looked over the dripping orchard at the garden, where the leaves of pole beans and tomatoes hung sodden. She couldn't see the pond from here but could imagine the gray dimpling water, the white parent ducks and their golden ducklings paddling out of the cattails, leaving ruffly v-shaped wakes.

She returned to the protection of the bear and brooded. One thing you learned from reading. Fairy tales, tales from *The Arabian Nights*, tales from Street and Smith, or *The Alhambra*. You were loved if you were beautiful.

" 'Beauty and the Beast'?" she said to herself. "Well, answer me this . . . would Beast have loved Beauty if she'd been Ugly or even Not-Bad-Looking?" The heck he would. Beauty had to be beautiful or no love story. No *love*. The ugly duckling had to turn into a swan, and until he did, his life was just not worth living. Whoever heard of a youngest daughter, mermaid or no mermaid, who was *plain?* "Not-Bad-Looking and the Beast"? Hah! Whoever heard of an ugly daughter who was not the eldest and wicked?

She knew she wasn't ugly. Plain. Too short. Not ugly. Clever.

"Be good, sweet maid, and let who will be clever."

Trixy Allen, one of her three best friends in In-wood, had written that in Ivy's autograph book, just before the move downtown. Ivy wasn't sure how to take it and didn't think Trixy knew how she meant it. Really, it *should* go, "Be beautiful, sweet maid, and let who will" and so on.

Trixy. Anne Pressman. And Connie. Connie Moore, friends of friends, the best she'd ever had. They'd visited at each other's apartments, sometimes staying overnight. Connie had a room all her own, but when she came to the Larkins', Francis, hardly grumbling, slept in Ivy's bed, and the extra folding cot was put up so that the two girls could use his room. She and Connie had read all the Oz books together, out loud, acting the parts with their voices.

Sometimes they'd walk down to the Cloisters, that medieval monastery perched over the Hudson River. They would stroll there, past tapestries and carvings and noseless stone statues in niches. They'd sit together in the garden of Saint Guilhem and speculate about the future. Their future. Connie thought maybe she'd be a nun and always got a holy look in that garden.

Those had been the good times, the good days. They had said they'd keep in touch, she and Connie. And Trixy and Anne. They would telephone and ride the subway uptown or downtown to visit each other. They hadn't. Even if they did, it would never be the same.

How could anything be the way it used to be, now that their mother had *decreed* that they should move from where they'd been happy (she realized now that she had been very happy in Inwood, even if she hadn't recognized sufficiently *how* happy when she was there), where they'd had friends and gone to a school that didn't make her feel that what she wore was more important than what she learned. "And why are you after thinking so, young lady, when you haven't begun the school year yet atall atall?" said her father in her mind, and she answered him glumly, "I just *know*, and that's all about it."

She had not confided her apprehensions to her father, because it wouldn't do any good. Pop, she knew, would defend her against the world, but not against Mama.

"I don't know what the situation was in *your* den," she told the bear, "but in ours, it's Mama Bear who calls the tune, and the rest of us who dance to it."

How could she fit into that school, how make a friend there? All those cashmere sweater sets, with *pearls*. All those braces on their *teeth*. That "Twelve Dancing Princesses" air the girls there had, just walking from one class to another. They were privileged, the sort of girls who would grow up charmed. The swans.

Oh, really—it was enough to make a person cry.

Ivy tried, sometimes, to face a future she was sure would not include someone to love her who was not a close relative. Already the girls she knew were sorting themselves (or being sorted) into those who were noticed by boys and would one day have people "stuck on them" or even "in love" with them, and those who would be ignored. Or, with luck, "liked."

Being certain she'd never be loved was another

reason Ivy read. Pop said that people who read too much were ostriches sticking their heads in the clouds. He was that kind of ostrich himself. He said he got it from the spindle side of his family, his mother's people having been teachers or priests.

Reading, Ivy forgot herself and thought about the people in the book. Almost *became* them. Jo. Jeremy. The Little Mermaid. The Little Lame Prince. Huck Finn. Jack Hawkins. Sarah Crewe. They had problems, all of them, but those were *their* problems. You could follow them, care about them, but when the book was finished, so were the problems. Unless you read it again, as she often did, oddly hoping that maybe this time Jo would marry Laurie, as she should have. That Mary, Jeremy's plain and awkward sister, might find a friend, as she should have. That the Little Mermaid, youngest of the sea king's six daughters and most beautiful of them all, as youngest daughters of course were, had never seen the handsome human prince, as she should not have.

She turned to her stomach, buried her face in the bear's gritty fur, sat up coughing. There was at least one positive thing to be said. She'd gotten through three days now without actually irritating anyone, even Geraldine. What her father would call a nugatory triumph.

The Larkin children adored the farm, cherished their two weeks here above all else, even Christmas. Loved the animals—Violet and the cows, the ducks with their far-from-ugly ducklings, Mousetrap and Ranger and that cocky cock with his seraglio. They loved the fields that they ran through, the brook where they swam, the rain, the sun, the flowers, the fruit, the day, and the falling dusk.

But.

Megan and Francis gave their hearts first to the family. To Uncle Jim, with his weatherworn face, who sat at the head of the table in the evening, looking as if he wanted their conversation when he really wanted to go to bed. To Aunt Tess, stumbling around, getting in the way, usually grouchy but never made to feel a nuisance. To Geraldine, beautiful and boy-crazy, doing her best to ignore the visiting relatives, except possibly Megan. And to Aunt Anna. They gave their love to Aunt Anna, dear and cheery and kind, who invited them up year after year and made them feel wanted.

"I love her, too!" Ivy mumbled, clutching a handful of dry fur. "I do!"

But.

She would have wanted to be on this farm if she should wake one morning to find they'd all disappeared, the whole family, leaving her to the animals, the fields of clover and Queen Anne's lace, the brook and the barn and this bear in the loft. She supposed that somehow they knew this. They couldn't love her as she wanted them to, because she couldn't love them enough. And what was there to do about that?

There was nothing to do about that.

"Ivy!" Megan's voice came from the barn floor below. "Ivy, are you up there?"

Ivy walked to the ladder and called, "You be careful, climbing. Want me to come down and help?"

"You better, maybe. Edward's with me."

"You're wet," Ivy said when she'd gone down the ladder. "Both of you." Edward was dressed for the weather. He had a wardrobe made by their mother, who owned a sewing machine and could make easy things like curtains and bear clothes. Today he was wearing a little raincoat. Ivy recognized an old one that Frank had torn past repair climbing alley fences with the Fregosi boys up on Broadway. "I see Edward had sense enough to put on his raincoat."

Megan smiled, then frowned. "I came out to be with you."

"That's nice."

"One of those men is in the kitchen. One of the hoboes."

"Want to sit on my bear?"

"Oh, yes. You carry Edward, please."

Settled on the rough brown fur, Megan removed Edward's raincoat. He was wearing gingham overalls that matched their bedroom curtains at home.

"Aunt Anna is giving him sandwiches and coffee," Megan went on. "And doughnuts. We've been making doughnuts. Scrumptious. You should've stayed with us."

Ivy's mouth watered. The fragrance, the crispness,

the sweetness of Aunt Anna's fresh hot doughnuts! "I hope there'll be some left for me."

"We made lots. But he's *very* hungry. After he's finished eating, he's going to split wood. He wants to do something to repay, he said, and of course there can never be too much firewood on the place," she said, sounding just like Aunt Anna. "Francis is going to watch. Aunt Anna says next year he can use the ax if Uncle Jim teaches him, but not this year. Geraldine is mad."

"Angry," Ivy corrected.

"That's what I said."

Geraldine said her mother was a soppy sap and a fool, and didn't she know that these tramps left signs on people's fences to show who was a pushover for handouts, and why did her mother think they *got* so many raggedy bums coming around begging at the back door and some of them even at the front door. . . .

Aunt Anna, each time, said in her clear, soft voice that she was ashamed of Geraldine for speaking so, that the men preferred to be called hoboes, not bums or tramps, which most of them weren't, that most of them were willing to work for what they got, that all of them were hungry, and that she would not turn hungry men away from her door, so Geraldine could keep her opinions to cool her porridge with. Geraldine went right on protesting, though the first time she'd done it in *front* of one of the hungry men, even Uncle Jim, who never got angry, this time did.

Geraldine, Ivy said to herself, has the face of the youngest sister and the heart of the eldest.

Why were so many men going around the country asking for food at the back doors of farms, singing for coins in alleys in the cities, traveling the roads, roofless, rootless, and hungry? Pop said it was because of the Depression. Ivy wondered where the hungry women were. Or the children. She'd never seen a woman come to Aunt Anna's kitchen door, offering to chop wood (maybe bake a cake?) in exchange for sandwiches, coffee, and some doughnuts. Now that she thought of it, she had seen children standing beside what her father called the *desperate troubadors* as they sang in the alleys for pennies or nickels.

"You won't lose your job, anyway, will you, Pop?" she'd said to him, and then wished she hadn't because she'd expected him to laugh and say of course not, but what he did say was, "God, I hope not."

SIX

UNCLE JIM DROVE HIS FAMILY into town on Sundays for church. He waited outside, reading his newspaper, while they attended services, his old Chandler parked in the shade of a wineglass elm near the churchyard. Uncle Jim was not a Catholic, and Aunt Anna said it didn't matter, he was a good man.

"Will he go to heaven?" Megan asked.

"He certainly will. If he doesn't, Somebody's going to hear from me, of that you can be sure."

When Aunt Anna spoke so, no one could doubt that Uncle Jim would get to heaven with the rest of them.

Megan was satisfied with the answer. She had happy notions about heaven, managing somehow to overlook the part about dying first to get there. Ivy thought her sister's picture of paradise was of a tremendous farm with all the animals in the world there, and all the people she loved, including her non-Catholic Uncle Jim and her no-longer-Catholic father.

Mr. Larkin was a cradle Catholic who had lapsed.

"When did you *stop* being a Catholic, Pop?" Ivy had asked.

"When I decided I wasn't a sinner."

"Do you have to be a sinner to be a Catholic?"

"No point, if you're not."

"But you're saying that Mama and Aunt Anna and Aunty and we three, we're all *sinners?*"

"Hardened, I should think, considering how often you're to be found in the confessional or at Communion."

"Pop!"

"Just kidding, Ivy, honey. *I* don't think you're sinners, but I'm not the one to decide, am I?"

"Why do you come to church with us at Christmas and Easter?"

"Recollections of my pious boyhood, I guess. A kind of longing, possibly. In many ways, it's such a grand religion. Beautiful and dramatic. Very comforting, for those that have it."

"Maybe if you looked inside yourself, Pop, you'd find you haven't really lapsed at all."

No reply. Just that wonderful quick smile. Pop often said that Mama's smile could charm birds. Ivy thought his could charm angels.

"Don't you like Father Cusick?" she had persisted. "I think he's awfully nice."

"A broth of a fellow. No, I mean it. . . . I'm not teasing. I like him. He puts me in mind of an Abbé Mugnier, who lived in Paris at the turn of the century. When asked if he believed in hell, he said, 'Yes, because it is a dogma of the church. But I do not think there is anyone in it.' "

"Oh, that's lovely."

"So you see, I have respect, even affection, for Father Cusick and priests the likes of him and the Abbé Mugnier. Father Cusick, indeed, strikes me as just the sort of pastor needed in a rowdy parish like his. A kind of celestial flatfoot, that's how I see him. Wits about him every second, and a sanctified shillelagh to use when need arises."

Ivy had decided the time was right to return to a matter she broached now and then, never successfully. "If that's how you feel, *why* can't we go to a parochial school? I don't *want* to go to that private school. Every time I even think about it, my heart falls into my stomach."

He'd immediately got that blank statue stare that meant no argument would reach him, far less move him.

"You could at least explain!'" she had shouted. "You aren't fair!"

"I will explain to you children, Ivy, anything I find myself able to explain. This is a matter I'm unable to. Yet, anyway. I'm unreasonable and I can't even explain that. I just don't want you to go to a parochial school. And I'm sorry you feel so about the school your mother's found, but you'll just have to give it a chance, for her sake."

"And what you two say, that goes for us."

"Unfortunately for you, yes."

Oh, they had the power, the adults. They piped the tune.

Ivy had two loves. The Catholic church and the New York Public Library. They were her refuges, where she found what the Middle Ages had called sanctuary. Once you reached sanctuary, nothing could harm you. Certainly not reality.

The library had the holiness of books, the church of ritual. She loved the odor of the musty stacks, the whispering voices, the little desk lamps in the one, the smell of wax and incense, the hushed Presence in the other. The church was more beautiful, of course, with a lofty, shadowed mystery. The mystery of the altar, of the slanting banks of votive lights flickering in their red glass cups, of the bell at the Sanctus. On sunny days, light poured through stained glass windows. "Waterfalls of color," Pop said someone had described it.

Ivy's faith was firm. She knew that His eye was on the sparrow and also on herself. If sometimes she wondered how this could be, there was the comfort of asking a priest—Father Jerold in Inwood, Father Cusick down here. They said that God could see all over the world as easily as she could turn a marble in her hand and see every detail of it. Once she had pointed out to Father Jerold that even with something as small as a marble she couldn't see *all* of it at the exact same time. "I can't see the other *side* of it, Father Jerold," she had said in catechism class. But he had quietly pointed out that she must not think that God's eye was limited, as was the eye of a child studying a marble.

She knew that His mercy was infinite. If she wondered now and then, and she did, why God let some people suffer horribly and other people appear to have *all* the luck, the priests could answer her.

In Inwood, a boy they all knew had been struck by a car and had his leg torn right off—or anyway, the doctors had to take it off. When Ivy had rather angrily inquired of Father Jerold as to the mercy in this, he'd reminded her that Peter had been spared his life. And that, of course, was so. Sometimes God visited afflictions upon us to test us, Father Jerold had explained, the way he had tested poor Job, who, after all, Ivy thought, came out of it pretty well. There were other examples in the Bible of God's mysterious ways, like the man who'd been bitter because his cow had died, but then learned that originally it was his wife— his son?—who was meant to be taken, and that the cow was a last-minute substitute, so naturally he wasn't angry anymore.

For the most part, she took her faith without question. Both Father Jerold and Father Cusick gently reminded her that she could not know God's mind, or His intention, and that much she did not doubt at all.

Confession bothered her sometimes.

"Bless me, Father, for I have sinned I haven't been

to confession for three weeks I was rude to my mother I used bad words I yelled at my brother—" She would rush through, breathless, wanting it over.

Last time, Father Cusick had said, before letting her go with an absolution and a light penance, "Nothing more, my child?"

How had he known? Something in her voice? He couldn't see her, could he? It was so dark in the confessional. Of course, his eyes had probably adjusted to it by then. There'd been at least six kids ahead of her. But he had so many children coming to confession, trying to race through and get out without too many prayers for penance. He couldn't tell one from another, could he? How had he known she'd been keeping something back?

Well, he had known, so of course she'd had to tell. In the dimness of the confessional, she had made an awful face. The first time she had a real sin (was it a sin?) to give him, and she had not been able to speak.

"I'm waiting, my child," the priest said. "Go on."

She'd burst out, "I have impure thoughts!"

"Oh? And what do they consist of?"

"I—I think about people with all their clothes off!"

Had she heard a gentle laugh? In a moment Father Cusick had said calmly, "That is not impure, my child. It's natural, at your age. At other ages, too. Nothing to worry yourself about. Anything else?"

"I lied," she had said automatically. Actually, she did not lie often, or seriously, but her confessions always seemed to her so meagre that she tossed in lies to plump them up. "No, I didn't," she'd added hastily. "Except now. I mean, *saying* I lied. I only said it because—" She'd stopped. She was getting too mixed up.

"That's good enough," Father Cusick had said. "Three Hail Marys and three Our Fathers." He'd given her absolution, and she'd gone forth to sin no more maybe. Well, to try not to.

He was such a nice man. She wondered if he didn't get bored, listening to the confessions of children.

Here at the farm, she did not confess or receive Communion. She and Megan, wearing their straw hats with the ribbons that hung down the back, carrying their prayer books, sat between Aunt Anna and Aunt Tess (Geraldine in a different pew, with some of her friends) and waited while their aunts went down the center aisle to kneel at the communion rail to receive the consecrated wafer on their tongues, and returned by the side aisles, prayer-clasped hands to their chins, to kneel again and talk to God in silence.

Francis didn't even come into church up here. He sat outside with Uncle Jim, and Aunt Anna said that was all right.

Ivy wondered what they all asked for, prayed for, those kneeling grownups. She would move forward to her knees and put her palms together, lips against her thumbs. "Please, Lord," she'd whisper, "please, please make me tall. Make me good, but make me tall, too. . . ."

During the week, Uncle Jim sometimes let them drive the tractor with him, even Megan, who sat on his lap while she steered. They collected eggs that were slyly hidden around the barn and yard by the hens. They took picnics down to the brook, Ranger and Mousetrap trotting along. They swam in the pond with the duck families, lay in the grass looking up through the trees at clouds in their shifting shapes. Cat, camel, steeple . . . what could a cloud not be? Once they saw a red fox running along a stone wall at the top of a meadow where the cows grazed. They couldn't believe how small he was, hardly larger than a cat. At night they heard the whippoorwill, heard the fluttering cries of screech owls.

O world, I cannot hold thee close enough! wrote Edna St. Vincent Millay. *Oh, farm,* cried Ivy, *I cannot hold thee close enough!*

But it was the beginning of the second week now. Pop, taking Saturday morning off from work, would come up on the bus to Glens Falls to be met by Uncle Jim next weekend. On Sunday afternoon they'd go back to New York City. Francis said he didn't see any reason why they shouldn't ride back by themselves, same as they'd come up.

"Does it occur to you that Pop might like to get a couple of days away from the city himself?" Ivy asked. "You *could* think about someone besides yourself for a change."

The two of them were sitting on the veranda late on Monday afternoon. Uncle Jim had taken Aunt Anna to visit a dear friend who was sick. Geraldine had gone with her, sulking.

"Oh, boy," said Francis, pushing vigorously on the swing. "You do the same thing every time."

"Do what thing every which time?"

"Spend the last week here trying to make everybody miserable because you are. Except you don't make me miserable."

"You aren't?" she asked.

"Not really."

"I don't believe you."

"Suit yourself."

"You're trying to tell me you want to go back to New York City instead of being *here?*"

"I'm not trying to tell you anything. Nobody can tell you anything. I'm just saying I won't mind getting back. Boy, I wish I could go to school with the Murphy kids."

Francis had, of course, found another bunch of rowdies to be friends with. The Connor brothers in Inwood, that Fregosi bunch up on Broadway, now the Murphys of the Lower East Side. Francis was a natural belonger to a gang.

"Their school," Francis was going on, "has a swell basketball team that plays other public schools around the city. That'd be fun. Even if they have a basketball team at this Holland place, how'd I get to play? We'll be spending all our time riding back and forth on the Third Avenue El. Boy! What a rotten idea! Snobby, too. The day we were there, I felt like somebody's toe dirt."

"That's disgusting."

"Sure is."

"I didn't mean—oh, phooey." Ivy chewed a little on the inside of her mouth, a habit she had when nervous. "Frank," she said, "why don't we just go up there and start failing everything?"

"Cheat backward? I bet it wouldn't be as easy as you think."

"We could try. Then they'd throw us out, and we could go to school a couple of blocks away and not have to ride the El. We'd save carfare." She sat brooding. "Mama's not fair, you know. Moving us down to that awful apartment because she thinks we're going to be high mucky-mucks because we got into a private school. She's a snob, that's what—"

"You cut that out! You're always picking on Mama."

"I am not. I'm only saying—"

"She doesn't want us to be high mucky-mucks. She thinks we're going to get a—a good education there. She's trying to improve us."

"*Her* way. Always her way!"

"She's the grownup, isn't she? How do you know she isn't right? I think she *is* right, and I want to get a good education. Better education."

"You just *said*, two minutes ago, that you wanted to go to a public school!"

"Well, I've changed my mind."

The back screen door slammed. Aunt Tess, followed by Megan, went stumping along the path to the barnyard gate, where the cows were crowding for entrance.

Frank stood. "I'm going to help with the milking. Aunt Tess says I have a farmer's hands." He studied her a moment. "Come on, Ivy. We can feed the cats."

She shook her head. Even for the cats she would not willingly endure the hostile presence of Aunt Tess. Hostile to her, that was. And she was very put out with Frank's way of switching positions practically in midsentence. You couldn't rely on anybody.

She'd have liked to watch the cats. They came with the cows, morning and evening, and waited for Aunt Tess to squirt milk in their direction. They'd stand with their pink mouths open, catching the milky streams she aimed at them. It was sweet to watch. Barn cats were wild, but Megan had got the mother to accept a gentle stroking. She was working on the kittens now. But with only six days to go . . .

Six days. A week from this minute they'd be back in that dark courtyard apartment, with a year to get through before they saw the farm again.

SEVEN

IVY TOOK A DEEP BREATH, got up, and went in the house. Quiet. Quiet as she had ever known it to be. A few old-house creakings. The ticktock of the Seth Thomas on the wall.

She waited a moment, then crossed the parlor and climbed the stairs. Her footsteps made no sound on the thin carpeting. Mousetrap was at her heels. He did not condescend to visit the barn for handouts, like a hobo. He was a house cat. Superior.

Turning toward the sewing room, Ivy halted at Geraldine's door, heartbeat quickening. With everyone out, why should she not—

Mousetrap wouldn't tell on her.

She went to her cousin's closed door, turned the knob gently, and stood on the threshold, as far as she planned to go. She had seen into this—sanctum—from time to time, when Geraldine forgot to close the door. She had never been in it. What would it be like to have, all to yourself, a room like this one? She stared around, eyes wide, so as to miss nothing.

Two braided rugs, mostly green and yellow with some white strips. A white iron bed with a yellow ruffled bedspread. Pillows encased in ruffled yellow slips. A French doll with long skinny legs and a prissy painted face lay propped against the pillows. There was a white wicker rocker between two windows that had yellow eyelet curtains with daisy tiebacks. The window shades were scalloped, with fringes. The lamp beside the bed and the one on the bureau had pink silk shades with fringes.

Geraldine had a dressing table with a ruffled yellow skirt and a lot of snapshots tucked into the frame of the mirror. Ivy moved into the room to see the pictures. Mostly boys, young, handsome, smiling for the camera and for Geraldine. One gorgeous fellow on a tractor. Bare muscular arms, white straight teeth, curly black hair.

Did those powerful arms ever go around Geraldine, pulling her close, holding her tight? Did that mouth press against Geraldine's lips, and did he say things to her? "You're beautiful, Gerry." Did he ever say, *"I love you"*? What would it be like to have someone who looked like this say that? To have someone like that hold you tight against him?

Ivy felt as if she were melting.

She looked at the snapshot for a long time, wishing she could take it. She would put it in *The Harp-Weaver* by Edna St. Vincent Millay, which lay on the table at home between her bed and Megan's and get it out at night before she went to sleep and look at him and think . . .

Oh, think *what?*

She had never seen this boy around here. Was he someone Geraldine had got tired of but not enough to throw away such a picture? Had he got tired of her? It would be nice to think of somebody throwing Geraldine over. "Sorry, Gerry, you turn out not to be my type. I like short, brainy girls who read poetry."

There were some bottles and cold cream jars and lipstick cases on the dressing table top. Ivy picked up an orangy Tangee lipstick, worn down lopsidedly, like a candle. She removed the stopper from a little blue bottle with a silver label and sniffed. Lovely. Simply lovely. Evening in Paris. She took the lid off a box of Coty's face powder and smelled that, too.

Mousetrap began to scratch at the rug. Ivy turned to stop him and saw her cousin in the doorway.

For a moment, silence. But Ivy knew she had to try for an excuse. "I didn't mean anything!" she said shrilly. "I didn't *touch* anything. Not really. I only—"

"You gruesome little snoop. Is this what you do when our backs are turned? Sneak and snoop? Well, I want to say, you don't surprise me! Not one *bit*, you don't."

"No! I never! This is the first—"

Geraldine was gone, running down the stairs.

Ashamed, afraid, sick, Ivy crept after her. How bad *was* it, what she had done? She tiptoed near the kitchen door. Geraldine was in there, yelling.

"I want to tell you, Ma, that I am sick and tired of having the poor relations dumped on us every summer!"

"Stop it, Geraldine. I will not have you talking that way about your cousins. They are members of our family, and—"

"They're sneaks and snoops, that's what they are."

"Geraldine! That's a dreadful thing to say!"

Ivy, cringing out of sight, thought, So it really was terrible, what I did. Wrong, of course, to go into Geraldine's room. She knew it was out of bounds. But she hadn't understood, until Aunt Anna got so upset, how *dreadfully* wrong it was. She hadn't taken anything, hadn't really touched anything. Well, just touched. Smelled the things—

She was shamed, her skin hot and sweaty, her knees shaky. No chance ever to put things right.

"I caught Ivy up in my room," Geraldine was telling her mother. "Going through my things. What do you say to that?"

Liar! Liar, liar, liar! *Not* through your things—

"Gerry, you must have misunderstood. Ivy wouldn't—"

"Ivy did. What was she doing in my room at all? I mean, is there no place that's safe from them?"

"Well—"

"I can't stand her. Look, isn't there some way we

could have the others and not her? I mean, Frank's okay, and as far as I'm concerned, Megan can live here. But that Ivy is just too much, I tell you."

"You seem to be telling me a lot of things," said her mother, "that sound very odd. I'll speak to Ivy—"

But Ivy was gone, running through the field. She ran until her side hurt, then dropped behind the protection of some blackberry bushes and lay shivering, watching the house until lights went on in the kitchen. Dusk began to gather over field, farm, barn. Kneeling on the rough grass, she leaned over, arms clasped tight as if to contain the tumult and pain inside her. Like a much younger Ivy, she whispered, "Mama! I want my *mother*. . . ."

She wanted to run away, get somehow to the bus stop and go home and never see anyone here again.

There was no way. She was trapped.

Down there, everybody was walking around, calling her. She saw her uncle go into the barn. He stayed long enough to have climbed to the loft and looked in every part of it.

Well, she'd have to go back, before Megan got frightened.

Rubbing her arm where she'd scratched it on the blackberry thorns, she started slowly down to the farmhouse, the place that she had loved more than anywhere else in the world, that now she had spoiled for herself, for good, for always.

She stopped and took some deep breaths. In a

70

moonless sky the stars were like blazing gumdrops. So far *away*, the stars. So indifferent to people, to pain. . . .

"Oh, *please*," she whispered, but not to the stars. Maybe to her mother.

"Where've you been?" Francis demanded when she sidled into the kitchen. "We been looking all over the place."

"Can't a person take a walk?" Did she sound jaunty, which was what she meant to sound?

"You had us worried," said Aunt Anna. "Supper's nearly ready. What did you do to your arm, dearie?"

"Nothing. I mean, I scratched it on some brambles or something."

"Go and wash it off, and I'll put some Mercurochrome on it. Mustn't take chances."

Ivy looked at her aunt searchingly as the Mercurochrome was applied, but the sweet-natured face looked the same as always. There was no way to tell if Aunt Anna knew or guessed that Ivy had listened to that conversation with Geraldine. If they don't know I heard, Ivy thought, then they don't know that I want to run away and never come back. And if they don't know that, they don't know how shamed and banished I feel. And if they don't know that—

She left off trying to puzzle it out, trying to make it come out as if it hadn't happened. It had happened.

Geraldine came into the kitchen and got the chicken pie to carry into the dining room. She had a stealthy smile on her lips, but she did not look at Ivy.

Uncle Jim, chewing a stalk of celery, said, "Figured you'd be back when you got hungry."

There was nothing in the atmosphere here that paid her unusual attention, except to be relieved that now they could eat.

It was easy to figure out. Aunt Anna had told Geraldine that she was not to say anything to anyone about Ivy's *snoopage*. Geraldine did what her mother told her to. So nobody knew what Ivy had done or what she had heard said about her. Except Geraldine. She knew.

Well, everything's ruined, Ivy said to herself, making herself eat, and smile now and then, and act normal. The joy of their time in the country was gone up in smoke for her. It did no good to realize that, as usual, she had lit the fire herself. She usually did start the fires that reduced her life to ashes.

In time, she'd learned from experience, something new came out of the ashes. No bright phoenix, but something to go on with.

She found, to her sorrow, that she was counting on her fingers the days she had to get through before she could leave the farm and go home.

PART THREE

EIGHT

AFTER SCHOOL, they rode downtown on the Third Avenue El to Chatham Square, then walked six blocks to home.

Francis would have liked to stay up at Holland to play volley ball. Or softball over in Central Park. Or rehearse to be in a play. He sort of fancied himself as an actor. He mentioned none of this to his parents. Francis, Ivy, and Megan did not talk about this school. They went, came home, did their homework, their chores, and in general behaved much as they had in Inwood, when they hadn't talked much about school, either. Mrs. Larkin, after the first couple of weeks, stopped asking questions. She knows, thought Ivy, that if we had anything good to say, we'd say it, and she isn't going to listen to anything bad we'd say, because that might force her to admit we don't want to be there. She's not going to admit that.

They moved between two worlds and, while they

were in the one, tried to behave as if the other did not exist.

Now Ivy, sitting on the El train next to her sister, lifted her eyes from *Tales of the White Hills* and waited pleasurably for the part where the car, leaning inward, went around a long curve before screeching into the station. It sort of reminded her of the roller coaster at Coney Island.

Megan never got accustomed to it. Every time, she closed her eyes and slid her hand into her sister's. Francis was at the other end of the car, at the front, watching the tracks, probably pretending to be the engineer. He had to ride with his sisters and look out for them because he was the oldest, because he was a boy, and because his father said so. "Doesn't mean I have to like it," he'd tell them, going off where nobody would know he was with them. At the same time, he kept an eye out. In case.

In case what? Nobody ever said.

He looked down the car, to be sure they'd observed it was time to get off, then stepped onto the platform and preceded them down the long skeletal staircase to the street. Carrying their plaid bookbags, his sisters followed.

Beneath the complicated elevated structure, a webbing of black tracery outlined by the sun lay on cobbled streets. Shadows cast by open tracks, by girders and pillars, were like the shadows of bones— bones of dinosaurs and mammoths and pterodactyls, long-vanished creatures that they'd seen at the Museum of Natural History.

New York City was full of marvels that people living on farms never knew unless they came to New York City. Once, a couple of years ago, when they'd been living in the big (bigger) apartment in Inwood, Aunt Anna had come to town with Geraldine and Aunt Tess. The Larkins had taken them all over, to the Cloisters, to Central Park, to the Bronx Zoo, to the museums on both sides of the Park. They'd gone back and forth on the Staten Island Ferry. They'd taken the subway to Coney Island and the Brooklyn Botanical Gardens. They'd seen Times Square at night and had gone around Manhattan Island on the Circle Line.

All the time they had been there, five days, Aunt Anna had been thrilled, Aunt Tess cranky. Geraldine had gone around with her nose in the air, as if it were all old hat to her.

As they walked away from the Chatham Square station, another train came roaring in overhead and screamed to a halt. The noise of New York was one of the things that had tried Aunt Tess's nerves, but the Larkins hardly noticed it. Ivy, now, was trying to decide whether to go to the library on their way home, taking Megan with her, or see her sister safe home with Mama and then walk the extra five blocks that would entail. Megan never wanted to stay in the library as long as Ivy wished.

Francis could take her. For once, he could take some respons—

He was vanishing up the street.

"Francis!" she yelled. "Frank! Hold up! I want you to take Meggy home so I can—"

"Can't hear you!" he shouted over his shoulder and disappeared around the corner with Johnny Murphy, who'd been waiting for him.

Ivy sighed, turned, and for an uneasy moment could not see her sister. Then she smiled and walked back to where Megan was adoring the iceman's horse, Valentino. He stood with one foot curved under, grubbing in his nosebag. He still wore his summer straw hat with the red paper poppy on it.

Finished eating, he rolled his eyes toward them over the nosebag. He looks, Ivy thought, flirtatious. Like an eastern lady with a veil, the sort she'd seen in her child's edition of *The Arabian Nights*.

Mr. Perine, the iceman, came out of the butcher store carrying his big iron tongs and whistling merrily. He had a heavy burlap sack folded on his left shoulder, where he rested the blocks of ice. Old and strong and gray and amiable, just like his horse, Mr. Perine was one of their favorite people.

"Ah," he said. "Valentino's lady friends!" His voice was always loud and cheerful. Mrs. Larkin said she didn't understand how Mr. Perine contrived to be so sunny, considering that crazy wife of his. Mrs. Perine had named Valentino long ago for her favorite movie star, Rudolph Valentino. He had died before Ivy had gone to a movie, but he'd been a famous matinee idol. Mrs. Perine put on mourning at his death and wore it for six months. "More than she'll do for me," Mr. Perine was said to have said. Mr. Larkin's opinion was that Mr. Perine didn't give a hoot if his wife wore mourning for a movie star, for a horse, or for himself. The Perines lived in the same building with the Murphys and had no secrets in the neighborhood because Mrs. Perine drank and told. Once, in a rage, she had thrown her gold wedding ring out of the window into the alley. Frank and the Murphy boys were still on the lookout for it. Not to keep, they said. For the reward.

Mr. Perine loosened the nosebag and tucked it under Valentino's chin. He turned to Megan. "Got his treat with you, right?"

Megan nodded, smiled, but did not speak. A tremor of—of tenderness, Ivy decided, *suffused* Mr. Perine's features as Megan took from her pocket a stick of twisted licorice she'd been carrying all day and held it toward the horse, who gently exposed his yellow teeth and chewed it in noisily. When he'd finished the treat, he allowed Megan to stroke his head from ears to nose tip.

"Feel," Megan invited her sister, softly caressing Valentino's nostrils, which seemed to quiver pleasurably at her touch. "Like velvet, Ivy."

Ivy patted the horse's nose and agreed that it was soft as velvet, though to her it felt squashy, sort of like a too-soft plum.

They walked on, past the pushcart peddlars with their gaudy displays. Ivy had noticed that there was a difference even in color between what rich and poor people wore. A pearl-pink cashmere sweater set on one of those girls she went to school with and a baloney-pink sweater like those swinging on hangers from a wooden rod on a pushcart were articles from different *planets*.

There was no Larkin money for suitable school clothes. Full scholarship did not cover expenses there, not with gym outfits to pay for, field trips to pay for, books to pay for. Lunch in the cafeteria to pay for.

Francis and Megan willingly and Ivy miserably had told their parents they would carry lunch in their old public school lunch boxes. Ivy, unable to prevent herself, had added that no one else did.

"Then it's out of the question," Mama had said. "I will not have you children embarrassed."

She doesn't understand anything, Ivy thought. Not one *thing* about what she's doing, sending us to that school.

"How much does lunch come to?" Mr. Larkin asked.

"We can get a sandwich and fruit and milk for a quarter," Frank said. "And in the middle of the morning they give us graham crackers and milk. Free. Elevenses, it's called."

"How very British," said Irish Mr. Larkin. "Well, kiddies, I guess we can manage lunch in the caff, for a while anyway."

There was nothing he didn't understand, and nowhere in the world, Ivy knew, was there a father to equal him.

But The Holland School was a wall that Ivy kept bumping into, bruising herself. It was out of the question ever to invite anyone home with her, as she had Trixy and Anne. And Connie! She hadn't heard from Connie in ages. She hadn't tried to get in touch with her. Emily Brontë, in a wonderful poem, had written:

> *Surer than that dwelling dread, the narrow dungeon*
> *of the dead,*
> *Time parts the hearts of men.*

And oh, it was true, it was true. A lot of writers claimed that love, friendship, could survive separation and silence. Ivy wasn't finding that to be so. Maybe, she'd think, friendship could survive separation, but not silence. Months of muteness seemed to erase memories, write a finish to closeness. At least, that was how it seemed to be with her and Connie.

Or maybe she was a person who could not really *be* a friend? That might be the reason she'd lost those in Inwood and had made none since.

Naturally, she never got invited to the homes of any of the girls from Holland. She pictured to herself their after-school gatherings, where they laughed and played records and experimented with makeup and practiced social dancing and made fudge and made fun of people who were not there. She contrived these scenes, shading and highlighting them, making herself ill. She had an active imagination. People said she got it from her father, but his was usually good-humored and merry.

I don't have a good-humored imagination, Ivy would tell herself irritably.

"Do you think I'm gloomy?" she asked her brother.

"I wouldn't call you a merry old soul."

"But would you call me gloomy?" she persisted.

A shrug. "You do seem to head straight for the darkest corner."

"All the *time*?" she wailed, willing him to deny it.

"Oh, well. A chink of light gets through now and then. I definitely heard you laugh one day last week. Maybe it was the week before. Tempus fidgets."

"You're just *trying* to make me miserable."

"Who has to try?"

In church, she would kneel and pray. "Holy Mary, Mother of God, make me cheerful. Make me be good company. Please. Make me tall, but cheerful, too. And I'll be good and serve you all my life. . . ."

She prayed to the Blessed Virgin, who would, she felt, be attentive to a girl's anguish. God, perhaps, would find her prayer petty.

NINE

AFTER BLOCKS OF DAWDLING, Megan and Ivy arrived home. At the courtyard entrance, Ivy said, "You go in by yourself now, okay? I want to get to the library before it—" She stopped, sighing, trying once again to understand what it was that Megan was afraid of. She'd been trotting along happily, talking about Valentino, wondering when he'd switch to his winter hat, hoping he had one. Now she stood staring at her sister, her expression at once stubborn and timorous, all her liveliness extinguished.

Ivy looked at the courtyard, which was maybe fifty feet deep. It was not an attractive place. Sunless, with gobbets of litter collected in the corners. But it was not, just now, in the daytime, *scary*.

"Now, look," she said. "Listen to me, Meggy. You have to take maybe a hundred steps from here to our door, in broad daylight, with Mama home and me here watching you, so what are you afraid of? What could *happen*?"

"I don't know." Megan's voice trembled, along with her chin. "Please, Ivy. Come with me."

"Okay, honey. I'm sorry. I don't mean to upset you. I was just trying to understand."

"So do I try."

"I know you do. Come on."

Mrs. Larkin was in the kitchen, singing as she cleaned the icebox. For a moment, Ivy stood listening, wondering how it was that her mother always sang when she was about the dreary chores of housework. *What* was there about housework that could allow a person to *sing?* Then she shouted, "Mama, I've brought Meggy home. I'm going to the library!"

"Fine. Don't be late. Don't stay too long. Where is your brother?"

"Last I saw, he was skulking around a corner with Johnny Murphy. As usual, I might add. He could, just once in a while, take Meggy home so I could—"

"What do you mean, skulking?"

"I don't mean anything. I just said it. No reason."

"Skulking means sneaking. Your brother is not a sneak."

"I didn't say he was."

"You just about did, and I want to know why. Is Francis up to something I should know about?"

"No!" How had she got into this? "Skulking's just a *word*. It sounds more—interesting—than just saying he's with Johnny. That's all."

"Ivy, words always mean something. If I haven't taught you that, your father must have. You'll get yourself in trouble, this way you have of saying the first thing that comes into your head without caring how it's going to sound to other people. You could *wound* someone, talking without thinking—"

"Okay. Now can I go to the library?"

Mrs. Larkin turned her head from side to side, fingers at her lips. She took her hand away and said, "Don't you understand at all what I'm trying to say?"

"I do. I really do, Mama. I'll be—I'll try to be careful."

"Well. Go along, then. Don't stay too late. If you do see your brother, ask him to come home, will you?"

"Sure." At the door she turned. "I really did listen, Mama."

"Of course. Have a fine time at the library. Onward and upward, as they say."

Outside, walking slowly, Ivy couldn't help thinking that sometimes it was onward and downward, though no one ever seemed to say that.

The library, her second sanctuary, was an old three-story stone building with grim pillars and worn wooden floors. It was solid, dusty, unchanging. A place to be trusted. Whenever she wished, she could walk down this block and here it would be. Hers. Anyone else's, too, of course. But hers.

Today she saw, with a start of dismay, that Miss Lerner was not at the desk. A stranger was there. As she approached, Ivy looked at the name on the three-sided wooden sign that always before had read: MISS I. LERNER. This said: MRS. V. HARGREAVES. Ivy could never guess the age of adults. They were youngish or oldish. Mrs. Hargreaves was youngish. Pretty. The only thing about her that mattered to Ivy was that she was not Miss Lerner, also youngish and pretty. And not here.

Ivy tried to smile at this powerful stranger, priestess of volumes. She put *Tales of the White Hills* on the desk.

Mrs. Hargreaves tapped her chin with the eraser part of her stamping pencil. "Enjoy it?" she asked.

"Oh, yes. I did." A pause. "Where's Miss Lerner?"

"She's been transferred."

"Oh." Ivy nibbled her cheek. "I see."

"You like Miss Lerner?"

Ivy nodded.

"Well, let's hope I'll prove a worthy successor."

Ivy nodded again, summoned a smile. She was used to Miss Lerner. Fond of Miss Lerner. She felt let down and hurt. You'd think Miss Lerner would have *said*, last time. She must have known she was leaving. Why hadn't she said good-bye?

"What's your name, dear?"

"Ivy Blaise Larkin."

"What a pretty name. I'm Mrs. Hargreaves."

"I know," said Ivy, glancing at the sign. Mrs. Hargreaves didn't seem to have anything more to say, so Ivy turned away and started for the stairs.

"Ivy?"

She turned back.

"The children's room is on this floor."

"I know that. I want something else by Nathaniel Hawthorne."

Mrs. Hargreaves nodded doubtfully, and Ivy went up, trailing her fingers on the wooden banister. It happened to her all the time. Because she was so small, people decided she was still a child. Can't they see? she asked herself. Do I *look* ten years old? Is my face a *child's* face?

When she came down, half an hour's browsing and debating later, and offered *The House of the Seven Gables* to be stamped, Mrs. Hargreaves lifted her slim dark brows. "I think we may be in over our heads, young lady."

"I won't be in over mine."

The librarian's amiable, amused expression snapped off. Scrambling after her mistake, not wanting to get on the wrong side of any librarian, Ivy said, "I didn't mean it that way. Not the way it sounded. But I'm fourteen years old, Mrs. Hargreaves."

"Oh? I thought—I see." She stamped the book, handed it over. "Let me know how you make out." Sink or swim.

"Oh, I will. I'll be sure to tell you."

She doesn't care how I make out, Ivy thought on her way home. But at least she isn't pretending to. Like Miss Lerner, who had acted so interested in her but hadn't bothered to say good-bye.

Upstairs, in the stacks, she had started *The House of the Seven Gables*. It was the best title she'd ever seen, and she did not think it was going to be over her head. But why had she *said* that? *Couldn't* a person sound a thing in her head before saying it? Apparently she couldn't. Her mother was right about that. Day by day in every way I'm getting better and better? Ha!! A lot Dr. Coué knew about life.

TEN

————————

"The family," Jack Larkin told his, "is the basic reality of life . . . human and animal and, in most cases, bird." An aspect of his view of family life was that his children would not wander around nobody-knew-where with nobody-knew-who. He always knew where and with whom his daughters were. At school, at church, at home, in the library, and with each other.

Francis. Well, boys were harder to control, and Frank had been a gang-joiner from the word go. But Mr. Larkin knew the nature of the gangs his son ran with. The Fregosis and their bunch, the Connors and theirs—they'd been all right. Mr. Larkin had known where they hung around, generally what they were up to, who their parents were.

When they'd moved here to the Lower East Side, it took Frank less than a week to hook up with the Murphy clan. Exasperated but resigned, he accepted the fact that his father would stop around at Murphys some evening "for a talk."

"You mean to case them," he said to his father, who waved a dismissing hand. Unless the Murphys turned out to be public nuisances, there wasn't much chance that Frank would be forbidden to see them. If someone forbade Frank, he dug in his heels, spit on his hands, and prepared for battle. He could be reasoned with, but rarely commanded.

The Murphys passed, in a fashion, muster. They lived a couple of blocks away, and that was good. Like cats, boys of Frank's age tended to roam within a restricted radius.

Mr. Larkin reported to his wife that the Murphy apartment looked like a pig fair and that Himself was cursed with the failing. Still, Mr. Murphy was not an abusive drunk. A neighborhood disgrace, surely, who created something terrible every weekend, shouting and stumbling in the streets, dancing up the fire escape instead of coming in by the door as a man should, yelling out the window that he was a dying man, poisoned by mushrooms. He was a cross that the Murphys seemed sturdy enough to bear, and he did not mistreat his family.

On Saturday afternoons, Francis did not run with his gang. Saturdays, after his morning at the Department of Transportation, Mr. Larkin and his children did things together. Francis had no complaints.

In winter, when bitter winds and cold congealed the city like one of Mr. Perine's blocks of ice, or on gray rainy days, they played a variety of games. They read aloud together. They made up plays that were then acted out for Mama in the evening. In decent weather they went rambling around the city. One afternoon a month they went to the big swimming pool at the St. George Hotel in Brooklyn, where Pop had taught them to swim. In good weather, they had lots of choices. Rowing on the lake up in Central Park was one of the best. Afterward they'd walk through the zoo, buying hotdogs and root beer and Eskimo pies from pushcarts. They went to the museums, one on the east side and one on the west side of the park. Sometimes they went to Fifth Avenue and waited for a double-decker bus with an open top. They'd climb the curving stairs and ride the length of Manhattan and then ride back again. Once he took them to a baseball game at the Polo Grounds. Only Francis enjoyed it. Ivy and Megan were dazed with boredom, and Mr. Larkin's team lost. The hotdogs were good.

Mrs. Larkin usually declined to share these adventures, even if she happened to be off duty on a Saturday.

"A few hours to myself," she said. "That's what I need."

Just the same, on an occasional summer Sunday, she would agree to go to Coney Island. They rode the subway that at a glorious point rushed up from underground into the open to give them that first whiff of salt marsh and sea. Coney Island! The tumultuous roar of the surf, the roar of the rides, the screams of the riders, the shouts of barkers at their booths of unwinnable prizes. Kewpie dolls! No one they knew had ever won a Kewpie doll.

They walked the crowded, salt-encrusted board-walks, in the splendor of the barrel-organ music surging over the clang-clang of penny arcades and shooting galleries.

They did not, like the average hordes at Coney Island, take sandwiches and hard-boiled eggs and thermos bottles of lemonade to eat off blankets spread upon the sand. When Pop took his family places, they ate out. Long weenies encased in soft rolls smeared with yellow mustard. Thick glass mugs of root beer with creamy foam rising over the rim. They'd stroll on, licking fragile mountains of cotton candy. (Too pink!) Despite its rarity, Coney Island was not their best, not their favorite ramble.

On the last Saturday afternoon of October, Mr. Larkin came home shortly after noon and found his daughters in the living room, one reading, the other modeling a hippopotamus in clay.

"Where's your brother?" he asked, dropping a kiss on Ivy's bent head and sitting on the floor beside Megan.

Ivy heard but did not reply, not wanting to remove her attention from Phoebe and Hepzibah Pyncheon in their seven-gabled house. A story not over her head.

"At Murphys," said Megan. "Does this look like a hippopotamus, Pop?"

He took up the little figure and studied it from all angles. "I'll wager a mother hippo, seeing this creation of yours, would take it for one of her own and urge it into the Limpopo for its first swim. 'Come, son,' she'd say, 'let's go for a splash. I guarantee you'll love it.' "

Megan laughed and leaned her head against her father's side. He hugged her and said, "Ivy, go find your brother and tell him I want him home."

Reluctantly, Ivy marked her place in the book with the silhouette of a paper cat made for her last Christmas by Megan. "He won't be *at* Murphys. They'll be somewhere. Playing stickball or something. Pop, did you ever read this?"

"Sure did."

"Did you like it?"

"Very much. And it's the kind of book you reread later in life, with more understanding."

"But there's nothing wrong with reading it now?"

"Certainly not. Whoever said there was?"

"Oh—nobody that matters."

"I really would like you to scout up your brother."

"If he isn't back by lunch, I'll go look."

Francis showed up shortly, looking expectant.

Pop had four slips of paper ready. After lunch (very light because they'd eat again later) they wrote their preferences for the afternoon's excursion. Pop put the four slips in his hat and Frank (it was his turn) took them out and read them aloud.

"One. The Cloisters." He put it aside, took another. "Two. Staten Island Ferry." Took the third. "Three. Staten Island Ferry." And the fourth. He looked up, grinning. "Four. The Galway Races, begob."

Mr. Larkin lifted his shoulders. "Impractical, I grant. Well, we have a majority."

Had there been only one possible selection, it would always have been the Staten Island Ferry. If he did not become an actor or a basketball star, Francis planned to be a ferryboat captain and give them all free rides for life. (At Christmas and Easter, he did sometimes declare for the priesthood, an inclination the family took with a grain of salt.)

Now Pop went off to shower, singing. " 'On the *road* to Mandalay . . . where the flyin' *fishes* play . . .' "

Half an hour later he emerged in his gray pinstripe suit, his clean white shirt ironed where it showed, and blue polka-dot tie. His shoes were carefully dusted, but not polished. Polish showed up the cracks and worn places.

"Oh, my," Megan exclaimed when he came out of the bedroom and struck a waiting-for-admiration pose, "you are *beautiful*, Pop."

"Just spiffy," said Ivy.

"The cat's spats," said Francis.

"Enough! Praise from one's children is praise indeed, but let us not back into blarney. Let's go."

They walked beside the East River to Battery Park, past wooden piers where freighters from around the world were tied up to discharge their cargo. The tide was running oceanward, carrying scraps of garbage to the sea. By day, the river was not altogether beautiful.

But at night! Now and then, on summer evenings, the Larkins would walk to an abandoned pier near home and sit looking at Queens, lit up across the river, and at the river itself, magical in the dark. Tugboats went past, north and south, with green and white and red running lights reflecting in streamers on the black waters. They could hear men's voices and music from radios in the wheelhouses. Once they heard a dog bark from one of the decks, though they couldn't see him.

How could anyone guess how noisy and dirty this river became by day, when it was clamorous with the horns and whistles of watery traffic, spangled with trash, laden with barges and tugboats and sometimes sailboats running under power, and now and then even a canoe?

Smelly, exciting, wonderful river.

They walked beside it now, each separately lost in thought. Ivy and Frank dawdled. Megan held her father's hand, skipping now and then, turning to check on her brother and sister.

"Penny for them," Ivy said suddenly, and Frank held out his hand. "Oh, Frank, for Pete's sake. I don't have one."

"No penny, no sales."

"Do you ever think about anything but money?"

"Basketball once in a while. Food. Anything else?" He looked at the sky and scratched his head. "Nope. That's about it."

"What do you think about that school? You never say."

"What school?"

"Frank!"

He shrugged. "What's to think? We go there, is all."

95

"Do you like it?"

"It's okay."

"You don't mean that. You *can't* mean it!"

"Look, Ivy—you ask me something. I tell you an answer. If you don't like the answer, that's tough. But don't tell me I don't mean something when I just now *said* it."

"But how can you—"

"If you don't mind, I'd rather not spoil Saturday thinking about Monday, okay?"

"But if thinking about school can spoil—" she began, but her brother raced ahead, catching up with Megan and Pop. In a moment, Ivy ran to join them.

As usual, Frank was right. Why ruin today with thoughts of next week?

At Battery Park, on the tip of Manhattan Island, stretches of cankered grass were enclosed by iron railings. Benches, threaded through with wooden slats, were lined along the railings. On some of them men were stretched at full length, sleeping, or maybe passed out. Ivy noticed how her father's face seemed to lose expression when he saw these men, as if his thoughts folded in on themselves and left his features blank.

There were stone drinking fountains placed here and there, and the children had liked drinking from them, finding it sort of an adventure (adventure being where you found it) until the day Ivy had gone over to one and found that somebody had been sick into it. Now she averted her eyes from them, as her father looked away from the shabby sleeping men.

Iridescent pigeons strutted, bubbling like coffee in the pot, on naked pink legs. Sooty sparrows swooped on horse droppings. Squirrels raced over the worn grass, searching out the people—there always were some—who had come with bags of peanuts for the purpose of feeding squirrels.

Like a small gray coffeepot
Sits the squirrel.
He is not all he should be,
Kills by dozens trees
And eats his red-brown cousins.
The Keeper, on the other hand,
Who shot him, is a Christian and
Loves his enemies.
Which shows
The squirrel was not *one of those.*

Much as they liked squirrels, Francis and Ivy would not have shared peanuts with them. Megan would have. Megan spent her allowance on licorice for Valentino, on scraps to feed the cats in the alley in back of their building. Megan would go hungry to feed a hungry animal.

Just outside the entrance to the ferry building, a man approached Mr. Larkin. He had a stubble of beard and wore an old brown suit too big for him and shoes that had string to tie the soles on. When he got close, they could *smell* him. He pulled off his cap and looked at Mr. Larkin without speaking. Ivy thought her father was going to push on by, but he stopped, sighing, and reached in his pocket for a coin. He came up with a fifty-cent piece and hesitated. Probably, Ivy thought, he'd been planning on a nickel or a dime but had not, through embarrassment, taken time to feel for the proper size coin. He handed it over. The man's eyes widened, and for a second it appeared that he was going to hand it back. Then, sighing, too, he said, "Thanks. Thank you."

"You're welcome," said Mr. Larkin and turned to his children. "Come on, kids. We'll be late."

That was silly. They had nothing to be late for. If they missed one ferry, there was always another coming along. Pop just wanted to get away from the man.

"He's a bum," said Francis.

"Don't you be calling anyone a bum, *ever*. You hear me?" Mr. Larkin said angrily.

"Yeah, but—"

"You heard. If you have no respect for your fellow beings, do the decent thing and pretend you do." He was so excited that he said *daycent*, which was going some, even for Pop, Ivy thought.

"Yeah, but Pop—" Frank started again.

"Damn kids," said his father. "No pity in them atall. No compassion. Poor devil crumbling in front of his eyes, and all he can think to say is *bum*."

Francis, biting his lower lip, eyes filling, looked at his father defiantly, furious to be spoken to this way

98

in front of his sisters. Then, surprisingly, he said, "I'm sorry. I didn't mean it. I mean, I did, but I shouldn't of said it."

"I'm sorry, too," said his father with a deep sigh. "But there are things you don't—can't—know about yet, I suppose. And you're no different than any other young person. If you don't understand something, call it by the simplest, unkindest terms, and I suppose you can't help that. It's how people are at your age."

Not fair! thought Ivy. It's how some people are at any age and some people are not, at any age. Her father had to be really upset to say a thing so unjust. She said nothing, since when he was like this, contradiction made him worse.

She was relieved that Francis had recanted. Pop held that the apology was a character-builder. If so, Frank would need to build his character on some other basis. He was rarely sorry for anything he'd said or done, and he might have spoiled their whole afternoon. Between them, her father and brother could ruin things entirely for the rest of the family.

ELEVEN

Mr. LARKIN GAVE THEM each a nickel, and they went
into the ferry terminal. The roof was a glass and iron
sky high above the goings-on down here, where the
vast area was studded with booths selling little
replicas of the Statue of Liberty, felt banners painted
with the skyline of Manhattan, ashtrays with the
Chrysler Building printed at the bottom. Balloons and
flimsy scarves and cheap charm bracelets celebrated
New York City and its harbor. Nedicks was there,
with a boy in white cap and apron serving hotdogs
and that thin, peculiar-tasting orange drink that you
never got anywhere else.

Ivy drew a deep exhilarated breath. She supposed
it possible that life would offer, one day, something
more wonderful than this, but this was now, and this
was joy.

They pushed through heavy wooden turnstiles, worn
shiningly smooth from the touch of generations, and
waited at a set of tall grilled gates, closed now,

watching the arrival of the ferryboat *Dongan Hills*. Motors throbbed as it came into the slip, ground against great tarred pilings to either side, and slid, finally, to rest against the pier.

Down like a drawbridge went the metal ramp. Ferry attendants secured the boat to stanchions with thick ropes, pushed to either side the low, folding metal fence, and allowed passengers and automobiles to flow off and away.

Oh, the ferry, the ferry, the Staten Island Ferry! *We were very young, we were very merry, we had gone back and forth all night on the ferry. . . .* Ivy felt her blood fizz with excitement.

They had, at different times, ridden all the ferryboats. The *Gaynor*, the *Rockaway*, the *Knickerbocker*. Today, the *Dongan Hills*.

With a long cry of her steam whistle, the *Dongan Hills* announced her departure for the watery wilderness of New York Harbor. Once clear of the slip, it was five sea-going miles to the St. George terminal on Staten Island. The voyage took them past the Statue of Liberty, past Ellis Island, where, Mr. Larkin had told his children, he might well have landed with his parents except that they'd chosen to arrive in Boston, that home away from home for the Irish, when they'd left Ballyconneely behind them on that long-ago day. "Meself a lad of eight at the time and on fire to glimpse the New World."

Far out, a garbage scow was burning refuse. To Ivy, lover of mythology, it looked like a Viking funeral pyre. An ocean liner, long and impossibly beautiful, was coming out of the Hudson River, surrounded by tugboats. Small and bossy, they escorted her across the sun-crinkled waters.

At times they'd crossed when the waters were calm, but today there were waves sufficient to lift the ferry and put her down and send a froth of salt spray over her prow. The children stood with their father on the top deck, at the front, breathing with their mouths open so as to catch flecks of foam.

"Like crossing the ocean," Megan said. "Isn't it?"

"It is, it is," her father agreed.

"Pop," said Frank, "tell us about crossing from Ireland."

They always wanted to hear about that trip he'd taken as a lad. Each time he told it somewhat differently.

"I remember," he said now, "days and days of waves, with the sea raised over our heads by the moon and the wind, and a storm me poor mother made sure would be sending us straight to the bottom, and me old man saying over and over, 'How can the ship go down and you cousin to half the priests in Galway?' And the rain slashing and the wind, the wind! Still, there—it was not such a storm atall. Just exciting. . . ."

Seagulls worked the shining waves, hunting scraps, quarreling and shrieking. An airplane panted across the sky, and they stared till it was gone over New Jersey. And then they stared at the Statue of Liberty, which seemed to rise right out of the water, a green-stone giant woman.

"Well," Mr. Larkin said at length, "shall we descend?"

In the great main salon, a man was playing *"O Sole Mio"* on his flashing, pearly accordion. Usually Pop put a coin in the minstrel's cup, but not today.

In the center of the cabin was the refreshment booth. Ivy loved the word *refreshment*. It summoned visions of foaming root beer, oily bags of buttered popcorn, and of course—the hotdog! The hotdog was central to these Saturday afternoons.

When they had made their unvarying selections, Francis said, "What about you, Pop? You haven't got yours yet."

Mr. Larkin patted his stomach. "Full. I'm considering a diet, I've been putting on the weight so."

"Well, it doesn't show," Frank said crossly. "It's because you gave fifty cents to—to the guy out there. And that's not fair. Why should you go without because of—"

"Shut up!" Mr. Larkin gestured nervously. "Sorry, Frank. Keep in mind, though, *I* had lunch. That fellow may not have eaten since—who knows when he saw his last meal?"

"Geraldine says they just spend what they get on whiskey," said Frank.

"Your cousin Geraldine is a pretty girl with some highly unpleasant notions."

"Anyway," Ivy said, "we can share. You can have half my hotdog, Pop."

"And half mine," said Megan. "Half of mine!"

"You can have my popcorn," Frank offered.

"There now," said Mr. Larkin. "*I* have nothing to complain of, the sort of children I have. Tell you what, I'll have a mug of root beer and accept some of your kind offers and consider myself the luckiest of men."

They sat outside on benches in the sun and finished their refreshments, and then Pop told them about the island of Manhattan, bought from the Indians by Peter Minuit in the year 1606 for, it was said, twenty-four dollars, though Pop said no one knew that for a fact.

At St. George, the trolleys came out of the car barn to go up Richmond Terrace for miles. Red and yellow cars, with tan wicker seats going all the way across, so that the conductor had to swing along the ledge, holding onto the uprights, to collect his fares with a little instrument that bit the nickels right out of their fingers. They got an entire long seat to themselves, and they rode as far as the trolley went and then rode back again.

Staten Island was like the country. There were meadows and cattle, lakes and private *homes*, and even farms. Twice, long skeins of Canada geese went honking overhead on their way to the south. There were haystacks in the fields, and barns like Uncle Jim's, and a sweet country peacefulness.

"I'd love to live on Staten Island," Ivy said to her father, who said he'd like that, too.

"Then why don't we?"

He shook his head and didn't answer.

It was a wonderful day. In bed that night, Ivy closed her eyes, put her hands together, and said, "Thank you for the happiest day of my life."

She and Francis said their prayers in bed, but Megan still preferred to kneel. She was kneeling now, whispering for blessings on everyone in her family, on Mr. Perine and Valentino, on Edward, and on all the animals everywhere in the world.

Frank, when he'd been younger, had knelt to say his prayers aloud, sending petitions to the ceiling for things he needed, wanted, or thought might come in handy. When he'd got over mixing up God with Santa Claus, he'd taken to praying silently. Ivy had an idea he was still asking for things, but maybe not. And who was she to talk? This was the first time she could remember just saying thanks without adding riders about how God was to improve her disposition, or grant her inches, or in some way reward her in exchange for promises of good behavior.

"Thank you," she said again, and added, "Bless everybody."

A grand day—and there was still Sunday between her and Monday and The Holland School.

TWELVE

THEIR MOTHER'S DAY OFF varied from week to week. Once a month she had a whole weekend free. She spent part of Saturday with her sister Kate, and part of it happily alone. Sunday, after Mass, was housework time for everybody.

She was on her knees now, doing their laundry in the bathtub, scrubbing on a tin washboard. Presently she would empty the tub, fill it again to rinse, then again to be sure the soap was all out. She used a bath towel to cushion her knees against the floor tiles.

Ivy, finished with changing the bed linen, paused a moment at the bathroom door. Her mother was thin and strong and, just now, disheveled. She stopped scrubbing for a moment, swept her hair away from her forehead with the back of her arm, pushed her hands against the small of her back, then leaned over the washboard again.

The sight went to her daughter's heart. Nobody

else's mother at The Holland School leaned over a bathtub washing sheets. Oh, Mama! she cried silently. My poor mama!

Those girls at The Holland School, with their clothes and their careless lunchtime choices in the cafeteria and their cliques and their carelessly unkind comments filled her with helpless rage.

Ivy had heard Madge van der Wall say to her friend Faye Cameron, "My parents are thinking of taking me out of Holland."

"Why?"

"Mother says they're letting in all types lately."

"How so?"

"Well, have you listened to these new ones talk? I should say *tawk?*"

"Oh, *Madge.*"

"I'm not kidding. Mother says you let this kind in, who *knows* what'll be next."

They hadn't probably meant for Ivy to hear, but had made no effort to see that she didn't. I hate them, she thought. I truly, really hate them. Probably it was a sin to hate. If so, she wouldn't confess it, because no amount of confessing or pretense at contrition would make her stop.

She'd been studying in the handsome school library, in the next carrel over from where Madge and Faye were talking quietly and at the same time regardlessly, as if they tossed their words out low but without caring into whose ears they fell. She'd listened, spellbound, too shocked at the time to be hurt.

"That little one," Madge had gone on, "is adorable, of course. Madame Gaillard says *elle la beauté fatale, sans doute*. I don't doute it for a second. In ten years no one will even be visible around her, and I'm glad I'll be somewhere else."

"The brother's awfully handsome."

"Frank? A dead-end kid."

"*But* smashing-looking."

"As for our classmate Olive—"

"Ivy, and you know it."

"How could anybody name a child Olive? *Or* Ivy?"

"I have an Aunt Ivy."

"No relation to the spotted or herbaceous ivy, I take it?"

"Oh, come on. You don't know what this girl's like. You never even talk to her."

"Neither do you. Tawk to her, pet. Neither do you."

"She doesn't seem to want to. Talk, I mean. But I feel sort of sorry for her. She looks kind of dazed."

"Out of her element. C'mon, Faye. Time for Latin. Don't you think Mr. McClellan is *cuddlesome*-looking?"

Sounds of books being gathered together, chairs pushed back. "You going to Louise's party on Saturday?" Madge asked as they walked away in their blond poise, mercifully in the other direction from Ivy.

For a long time she sat, open books unnoticed, a familiar, hateful pain stuck somewhere, she thought, in her ribs.

She could bear—sometimes even like—to hear her sister praised. *Beauté fatale*. Okay, Megan had that.

Hearing about it did not affect her too terribly. But the other things those two had said—hateful, horrible.

Nobody ever praises you, you poor hopeless thing, she told herself. Praiseless you proceed, have proceeded, will proceed. Forever! No lady, seeing you, will stop on the street and gasp, "Oh, look at the little dolling!" No one even tells you you do your schoolwork well.

What is the *matter* with you, Ivy Awful Larkin?

She leaned her head on her hands. Really, she did feel awful. Sick. Clammy. Even her hands were cold. This pain inside her was absolutely dreadful, like something alive. Like an organ grinder's little ugly monkey holding out a tin cup, asking for a penny. She was like a little monkey holding out her cup, asking for a word, a compliment, *something* for her efforts.

"Oh, Pop," she whispered. "What am I going to do?"

She did her schoolwork *well*. She got good marks. But nobody ever *praised* her. Why couldn't her English teacher, anyway, hand back a book review, like the one she'd done on *Great Expectations*, with something besides an *A* on it? *Ivy Larkin, this is a remarkable piece of work, and I detect a future writer in you. Your choice of words, your insight into character, your—*

"Ivy?"

It took her a **moment** to turn, to hear Mr. McClellan's voice. "Ivy, are you feeling all right?" he asked. He sounded, she thought, sort of impatient.

Gathering her books together, swallowing hard, she got up. Head hanging, she mumbled, "I'm fine. I was just—I'm okay." Stumbling a little, she hurried away.

She ran for the El, just caught a train, and sat, not reading, trying not to feel, not to think. She just wanted to get home, where she was safe, where she was loved. The ride which seemed endless, ended, and then she ran and ran—toward home and love.

But now, watching her mother doing laundry at the bathtub, Ivy felt her heart harden. Traitor! You've done this! You've put me in that daze, and you won't even see what you've done! I hate you!

Mrs. Larkin sat back on her heels, glanced over her shoulder. "Finished with the beds, love?"

"Yes."

Mama was pretty. How did it happen that with the same basic equipment everybody's face came out different from everybody else's? What could be *done* with just two eyes, a nose, a mouth, a couple of ears, some hair, and the bones underneath it all? How did this variety come about? It was there, all right. Some people were pretty, some beautiful, most nothing one way or the other, and some were homely. Well, plain. Despite stories like the *Man in the Iron Mask* and *The Prince and the Pauper*, nobody had ever been the exact copy of somebody else in the whole history of the world. Even twins were never exactly alike. It seemed impossible, but was fact.

Mrs. Larkin began wringing out small articles and dropping them in the big wicker laundry basket that had been Megan's cradle long ago. Presently Pop, who was now pushing the carpet sweeper over the living room rug, would come to handle big things like sheets and towels. Then he and Francis and Megan would take the elevator upstairs to hang their laundry on the clothesline assigned to their apartment. Megan carried the canvas bag of clothespins to hand to her father and brother. Finished, they'd hang around on the roof for a while, just looking.

Ivy went into the kitchen and got the makings of meat loaf from the icebox. Mr. Perine had pointed out to them what a fine object their icebox was, the wood dark and nicely grained, and with real brass fittings. After that, Frank had kept the brass polished, and Ivy often looked at it with satisfaction. They owned something fine.

She chopped carrots and green pepper to put in the meat loaf. Carrots for eyes, said Mama. Green pepper for fine muscles. Nurses thought of things like that.

"Is there some kind of food makes a person grow?" she asked as her mother came in to check on her.

"Oh, honey. Don't worry so much about that—"

"You'd worry, if you were a dwarf."

"You are not a dwarf."

"Midget, then."

"Not that, either. You're a short girl. Lots of girls are short and love it. It's dainty."

"Nobody with short legs is dainty."

"Oh, Ivy—you exaggerate so. You really must stop it!"

"I do not exaggerate. Megan's got the same amount of stuff stuck on her face that I have—eyes and nose and ears and so forth—but she's everybody's beautiful baby, and I look like Squirrel Nutkin."

"For goodness' sake, stop whining, Ivy. Actually, you are a nice-looking girl with lovely eyes. If you just didn't *think* about yourself all the time. That *is* unattractive—"

Ivy turned her back, blinking angry tears. Ever since she'd started at this *poisonous* school, she'd had this awful, constant need to cry. Nobody understood. Nobody. Megan grew taller every day. Like a wand. Like a willow. Beautiful as a tulip. Megan did not think about herself all the time. Ivy wasn't sure that Megan ever thought about herself, except when she was frightened. And she did not speak without thinking.

She punched crumbled crackers into the meat-loaf mixture. That's what I'll do, she told herself. Stop talking. I mean, tawking. I'll read and think and won't say a word except that was some storm last night or there isn't enough catsup for the meat loaf. Things like that. Nothing to offend, nothing that matters, nothing about myself, ever.

"There isn't enough catsup to put in the meat loaf," she snapped. "To say nothing of last night's storm."

"What is the matter with you, Ivy? I think the devil gets into you sometimes. What has anybody said or done to get you snarling again?"

"I'm not snarling *again*. I don't snarl. Whine, yes. I'll give you whine. But *not* snarl." She pushed the meat loaf into an oval shape. A pound of ground meat, package of saltines, catsup (not enough), some chopped onion, green pepper, carrot, a stalk of celery, salt and pepper, some sage. She opened the icebox door, put the pan in for later cooking, closed the door, and turned to face her mother, who was not there.

Not in the living room, either, and the bathroom door was open. So she'd gone upstairs, to be with the others on the roof. When the laundry was hung, they'd lean on the parapet and look at the buildings of downtown Manhattan, at the bridges with their traffic and the river with its traffic, and the street below and all that was going on there. They'd be together, looking and talking, not noticing that Ivy was among the missing.

She went into the bedroom and lay down, one arm across her eyes, and tried to face herself. Ivy Larkin, without the Blaise. Ugly duckling, headed for ugly duckdom and whining all the way.

The apartment door opened, closed, and there was her mother, back so soon. She came in and sat on Megan's bed, waiting for Ivy to take her arm down. She did and turned her head on the pillow to meet her mother's eyes.

"Are you jealous of your sister?"

What a dumb question! Yes, I am jealous of my sister. Who wouldn't be? You can love someone and still wonder why there hadn't been even one wicked fairy at her cradle. Her laundry basket. The good fairies had fallen all over each other, sprinkling baby

113

Megan with gifts and graces. They hadn't been able to *think* of enough gifts and graces, so doubled those they'd already bestowed. And who, pray, had been at Ivy's birthday celebration? A cackling crone, looking, *sans doute*, like Aunt Tess.

But what about the wicked witch who'd stood at Megan's wicker cradle and said, "I'll put this splinter, fear, in her mind, and let's see her cope with that!"

"No, I'm not jealous of her."

Mrs. Larkin put her hand on Ivy's forehead. "Do you feel all right?"

"Feel fine."

"We thought we'd go to the movies."

"Okay by me."

"Are you coming?"

"Sure."

THIRTEEN

ONCE A MONTH, Aunty and Unk came for midday dinner. Aunty, who had a low opinion of her sister's cooking, brought the food and cooked in the Larkin kitchen. A chicken, a roast, at holidays even a turkey. There was always a homemade pie or cake and cookies for the children to eat during coming days. Aunty liked to cook and had plenty of time for it. She and Unk were childless. Ivy understood that for years this condition had grieved them but that now they were resigned. She and Frank thought "pleased" would have been a better word. They had all this freedom, and no worries, and could spend their money just on themselves. They did not do this. They were generous with their family, but they *could* have spent it on themselves. Ivy compared Aunty and Unk in their easygoing, affectionate life to her parents who were overworked, worried about money, often tense with each other. *Because they had children.* Why wasn't everyone childless?

Unk was a linotype operator on the *World-Tele-gram.* Aunty had never had a job. She was pretty and wore nice clothes that she tried to share with her sister, who wouldn't take them. Unk was the steady one in the family. He never raised his voice and never changed his mind. He was a Republican. When Alfred E. Smith ran for president and lost to Herbert Hoover in 1928, Unk had been quietly satisfied and Pop mad enough to tear up the sidewalks. This year, 1932, they were on opposite sides about Mr. Roosevelt and Mr. Hoover.

"You don't know yer head from a hayfork," Pop was shouting. "You think the Republicans are going to save yer perishin' job when the crunch comes?"

"It's not a perishing job," Unk said. He fixed his brother-in-law with a calm eye. "I *like* my job, Jack. Wish we could all say the same—"

"You listen to me now, Vince—"

"Jack, the day I listen to you will be the day Saint Patrick invites Cromwell upstairs for dinner. And another thing—"

"Ta dah!" Aunty sang out. "We're going to have a taffy pull! All hands fall in!"

When dinner was over, their father and uncle settled down to listen to a football game on the radio. When it was over, the four grownups would play bridge. Another part of the pattern of these family sociables.

Ivy, lying on her bed, licking her rope of buttery, molassesy, streaky amber taffy, looked up from *The Idylls of the King* and listened, briefly, to sounds from the living room. She did not think bridge was a game she'd ever take to. If you didn't know better, you'd think the people playing it were being *hostile*.

Was that what being grown up came to? Working, eating, washing up after eating, and winding it all up with a game of *bridge?*

Was it for the sort of life her family led that a person longed to be grown up?

FOURTEEN

THE GROUND-FLOOR APARTMENT, with the bars on its windows, gave Francis occasion to be witty. Opening the door, he would say, "I'm Sergeant Larkin. Park your valuables on the desk over there and don't try any funny stuff, got it?" Or he'd leap around the room, thumbs in his ears, fingers wagging, saying in a mosquitoey voice, "Welcome to the privacy of our Bedlam. I'm Napoleon and the rest of these people are crazy."

The bars were protection against dangers that probably did not, but might, exist.

"It's an interesting fact," said Mr. Larkin, "that this nation, destroyed by a depression from which there is no observable point of escape if we fail to elect Mr. Roosevelt, is now considerably less crime-ridden than it was when we were living in prosperity."

"When did we ever live in prosperity?" Francis inquired.

"That was a collective 'we,' embracing the United

States as a national glob, not taking individuals into account. But let me tell you something about this prosperity that's supposed to be right around the corner." He lowered his voice and looked around furtively. "*It is*. Only nobody's twigged it yet that the corner's the one we left behind us, not the one we're coming up on."

"Jack, stop it. Please," said Mrs. Larkin. "We have our jobs, don't we? We're lucky."

"Have I denied it now? I'm speaking in generalizations."

"Oh." She stared out the living room window, through the bars, across the street to Geety's Chemists on the corner and Goldberg's Grocery, where they did most of their trading and could run a bill. "It's turning cold," she said.

It was very cold for the end of October.

The bedroom windows faced not the street but the courtyard. They kept those blinds down behind the curtains all the time, shutting out the sight but not the sounds of that gray area. Day and night they could hear voices, footfalls, arguments, roller skates. Even the twittering of those pavement birds, the English sparrows, could be heard. When the wind was up, it moaned in the courtyard like a crowd of ghosts. An elderly couple from the fifth floor went out to a bar every Saturday night and came home in the early morning talking in loud, slurred, hostile tones. They usually didn't wake Frank, but Megan and Ivy would start out of sleep in alarm, before realizing what had awakened them. Then, for a while, they'd whisper together in the soft glow of the night-light before falling asleep again.

One night, after the drunken pair had stumbled noisily into the building, the sisters heard another sound, like a squeaky sobbing.

"What's *that?*" Megan cried out. "What's *doing* that?"

"How do I know?" Ivy asked. She went to the window, pulled the curtain aside, and lifted the blind, trying to see into the dimly lit courtyard. "It's underneath us. Right down here under the window. It sounds—hurt."

"Hurt?" Megan whispered. "Is it a person? Shouldn't we call Pop?"

"No. Wait a minute." She listened closely, holding her breath. "Meggy, it sounds kind of—it sounds like an animal. Whimpering." A puppy, maybe? A cat?

Megan was beside her, trying to look out.

"Are you two holding a séance?" Frank grumbled. "Can't you let a person sleep?"

"Are you awake, Frank?"

"Yeah. Leaping from branch to branch of a young oak tree."

"Come over and listen to this," Ivy said.

"I can listen from here, and I'd rather not. Will you please pipe down?"

"There's something out in the courtyard here, crying. Whimpering, sort of. I think maybe an animal."

Pulling his pajama strings tight, Francis shuffled

to the window and stood beside them, head tilted. "Jeez." He rumpled his hair. "What d'ya suppose we better do? Should we call Pop?"

"I'm going out there," Megan said. She pulled on her coat and sat on her bed to put her shoes on.

Her brother and sister looked at her in disbelief. They looked at each other. Their Megan was going to go out there to the courtyard, in the dark, to goodness knew *what*, without even asking anyone to go with her?

"Holy smoke," Frank said. "You can't do that, Megan. You can't go out there by yourself."

"You can come. But anyway—I am. Maybe it's hurt and frightened. Would you want to be all alone in the cold and crying and nobody doing anything about you?"

"Maybe it might bite," said Ivy.

"We better call Pop," said Francis.

"No." Megan stood up. "Pop'd take it to a policeman, and they'd take it somewhere and kill it."

"But if it's awful hurt—" Frank began.

"Maybe it isn't. Maybe it's just lonely and scared. We could find out. Then if—" She stopped, eyeing them with determination.

Ivy and Francis were getting their coats on over their nightclothes. She wasn't going out there without them. That she was prepared to was beyond comment.

"Better take a blanket," said Frank. "To wrap it in, in case it wants to bite or something."

They'd been whispering, and now, as they stole

121

through the dark apartment, they stopped speaking. Gently easing the door open, they stepped into the chilly, shadowed hallway, through the big front door to the courtyard.

It was terribly cold. Why did people think Hell was going to be hot? An eternity of motionless bitter cold was Hell, as Ivy pictured it.

Snow had begun to fall, and already the gray cement in the courtyard was thinly covered, as if with chalk, and the puppy, huddled in the corner underneath their bedroom window, holding one paw against his chest, was lightly dusted with white flakes. He cringed a little at Megan's approach, but his despairing cries lessened.

Megan crouched in front of him, her brother and sister standing back a little so as not to overwhelm him.

"Come on, dearie," Megan was saying. She sounded, Ivy thought, exactly like Aunt Anna. "Don't be frightened. We're here. We'll take care of you."

It was difficult to see in the murky snow-tangled light that came from the one globe above the doorway, but they could sense a slight forward movement on the puppy's part. "*There* you are," Megan said happily, and gathered him into her arms. Frank held out the blanket, then shrugged and glanced at Ivy. The three of them made their way back to the apartment. Their wild-eyed parents were on their way out.

"What the—what've you been up to?" Mr. Larkin shouted. "What do you think you're *doing*—"

"You frightened us!" their mother said, on the edge of tears. "You scared us terribly. What are you doing, coming in at this hour? What are you doing *out* at this hour? What's going *on?*"

Megan, cradling the shivering dog, gave her parents a bright, embracing glance. "Lookit," she said. "We went out to get him."

"She was going to go by herself," Frank offered.

"We heard him crying," Ivy said. "He was crying and crying out there. So we had to go get him, didn't we? And Meggy wasn't afraid at all. It was her idea."

"Jesus, Mary, and Joseph," said Mr. Larkin.

Mrs. Larkin sighed, pushed her dark hair from her forehead, and said, "We can't keep it."

Megan clutched the puppy closer and set her jaw.

"Look, honey," her mother said persuasively, "you must see that in our circumstances, an animal is—" She paused, altered her approach. "It would not be *kind* to this puppy to keep it in an apartment where he'd be alone most of the day. You want to do what's best for the animal, don't you?"

Francis looked at the living room windows beyond which snow was falling thickly and piling up on the window ledges. "Can't put him out in this, can we?"

"Oh, for goodness' sake! This is really impossible. All right. Put him—it is a him?—"

"Yup," said Frank.

"—in the bathroom for the night, and we'll decide what to do tomorrow. Look here, Megan—the SPCA would find him a good home, where he'd have the companionship he needs. Don't you see?"

123

"I want to keep him," Megan said. She so rarely expressed an opinion contrary to that of her parents that it had the effect of an ultimatum.

"But, Meggy—" her mother began. "Oh, let's drop it for tonight. Do you realize it's almost two o'clock? I have to be on the floor in five hours. Put him in the bathroom and tomorrow we'll—"

"He'll be lonely in there, all by himself."

"At least he'll be warm. And dry. Now, do as I say, and let's go back to bed. Please!"

Closed in the bathroom, the puppy set up his keening again, and then all at once was quiet.

"Now look what she's done," Ivy whispered to her brother.

"Okay by me. I just want to get some shut-eye."

Up before anyone else in the morning, Ivy gently opened the bathroom door. On the floor, on the bath mat, wrapped in a blanket with their heads side by side on Megan's pillow, were her sister and the puppy, peacefully slumbering.

She returned to the bedroom smiling and said to Frank, who looked a question at her, "We'll have to deflea both of them. I fear poor Edward's on his way to the back seat."

"Who's going to win, Meggy or Mama?"

"Well . . . I know one thing. If that dog goes to the SPCA, Megan's going with him. Do you think they'll find them a good home together?"

Frank grinned. "Just the same, do you realize that because of that puppy, Megan forgot all about being afraid? That time, anyway. Maybe he's her good-luck piece. He could be the *saving* of her, maybe. I mean, think about it that way."

"I do. Why don't you go say that to Mama? I guess plenty of other dogs in the world have to be alone in the daytime. Better than going to the SPCA, where they'd find him a good home, I don't think. He's an utter little mutt and wouldn't have a chance. Tell Mama that he'd get enough love when Megan's home to last him through the school day. Put it that way."

"Why me? Why don't you tell her?"

Ivy looked at him pensively. "Because you get along with her better than I do. She'd listen to you better."

For a moment, they thought he'd deny it. Then he lifted his shoulders and said, "Okay, I'll give it a try."

When he'd gone, Ivy walked to the living room and looked out. Beautiful. It was just beautiful. Snow falling lightly now, but during the night it had covered their mean street with a white concealing quilt. There were a few paths on the sidewalk where galoshed feet had trodden and, out in the street, the trail of Valentino, or some other horse, pulling his wagon. Now the milk truck, with chains on its tires, came rattling along and stopped in front of their building. The young milkman got out, pulled a wire basket toward him from the back, hesitated a moment, and glanced around. He stooped, gathered a handful of snow, and made a big snowball that he heaved straight up with an exultant air. Then he took up the basket and carried it, frozen cream caps thrusting up an inch or more out of the clinking bottles, through the courtyard and out of sight.

"Snow in October," Ivy said softly, aloud. "How lovely!"

She thought about the farm, probably covered now, too. Field and garden, house and barn. The air would be milk-white with falling flakes, feathery and flouncing. There would be icicles along the eaves of house and barn, and up in the cold deserted loft her brown bear would lie tamely snarling into the shadows. On the farm, she had no doubt, the snow would remain unsullied, sparkling in sunshine, bluish at nightfall, long after this in the city looked like dirty plaster.

Well, as Pop always said, seize the moment. . . .

Megan named the puppy Pickwick. He was affectionate, but did not confuse anyone else in the family with his rescuer. He gave his bruised heart entirely into Megan's keeping. Still, even after he'd filled out and apparently come to believe he was really home, he never lost his worried look. He remained afraid of sudden noises, lifted voices, other dogs, any cat, the elevator, and Mr. Perine. He appeared to feel that danger, or anyway some pretty unpleasant surprise, awaited him at every turning. Megan, constantly reassuring, seemed to lose her own fears without noticing. One night the bulb in the bedroom lamp burned out. For an experiment, Frank did not replace it and at the end of the week said to Ivy, "See that? I don't think she's even noticed."

"I suppose, with Pickwick at the bottom of the bed every night, she doesn't need it."

The two of them studied Pickwick, lying at the front door, waiting for Megan, who had gone across to Goldberg's, by herself, to get him a little bag of scraps that Mr. Goldberg saved for her every day.

"Told you he'd be her good-luck piece, didn't I?" said Francis with satisfaction. "But boy, is he ever homely. Pickwick," he said, "you are one really dog-faced mutt!"

Pickwick pricked up his ears, but did not remove his gaze from the door.

FIFTEEN

THE HOURS OF THE DAY spent at school—most of them from Monday through Friday—Ivy did not consider part of her real life, although there were aspects of Holland that she knew were forming now part of what she would one day consider "real" life.

Lessons were interesting. She *liked* to learn and to study. French was an unexpected treat, though Madame Gaillard was not. Madame had favorites. Despite doing her work well, Ivy had no illusions about becoming one of those. She enjoyed assemblies, where they sang or listened to music or to lecturers who came with slides to tell of the mysteries of other lands, other people, the skies, or the oceanic depths.

She was happiest in the twice-a-week art classes held in the sky-lighted studio on the top floor. The odor of paint and sawdust and wood shavings, the pungent scent of library paste, a sharp smell that rose when she plunged her hands into one of the deep wells of moist, cool clay . . . all that satisfied her deeply.

She showed no signs of artistic talent and did not think she had "latent ability." She just liked the studio.

"Latent ability" was a term much used at Holland to describe students proving slow to learn. No one was written off as actually "slow." Ivy supposed that was a good thing. Just the same, there were plenty of people at Holland who should not have their brains put on public display. Boys who could not think further than the next basketball game. Girls whose interests stopped at the next dress and the current crush. Most of the girls in the ninth grade were, like Geraldine, boy-crazy. Their every sentence began with "he."

Ivy, too, felt stirrings of the trembling, tentative, tormenting emotion. She had been in love with John Keats, Rupert Brooke, Cyrano de Bergerac, Sidney Carton. Lancelot, bruised and bronzed and enmeshed in a great and guilty love, quite weakened her. She could never, not possibly, have a crush on one of those callow Holland boys with their pallid city faces, their breaking voices, their adolescent swagger. She scorned them. I want to love a man twice my age, she told herself. A man with a *visage*.

She did not need anyone to tell her that loving dead poets and heroic myths was safer than chancing her luck with a live boy her own age.

Her brother and sister did not find the new school a stronghold to be assaulted every weekday morning.

Megan went along in her beauty, her *niceness*, drawing affection from everyone, teachers, staff, students, reserving her own affection for home. Megan's life centered in her parents, her brother and sister, Pickwick and Edward. At a slight remove were Aunty and Unk, Aunt Anna and Uncle Jim. That completed Megan's circle, with Valentino and Mr. Perine just on the edge. It isn't that she thinks to exclude other people, Ivy thought. She just doesn't take them into account.

Ivy took even strangers into account. If an eye lingered on her for a moment in the El, she would wonder how that person was seeing her, knowing the person undoubtedly wasn't seeing her at all. Terrible, she'd tell herself, helpless to change. This is terrible. *Caring* what Geraldine thinks of me. Or what Faye or Madge thought, or the art teacher whom she liked, or Madame Gaillard whom she disliked, or some woman on the El she'd never seen before and would never see again. Now, look here, she'd say to herself, it doesn't *matter* what they think. It mattered all the time.

Frank accepted Holland with good-natured indifference. Being poor among rich kids didn't trouble him. He even had friends among his classmates. No one he considered bringing home with him, but people he liked, who liked him. Frank's real life was with the Murphy boys. His gang. Besides, he enjoyed doing things with his family, something the Murphys considered beyond the bounds of credence. They were never seen with their parents except at church.

Francis went his way.

If the boys at Holland found it odd that he could never stay after school for extracurricular stuff, they got no explanation, nor were Johnny and Patch and Terence Murphy given reasons why Saturday afternoons were otherwise taken up. Frank said he'd read somewhere that you can do anything if you don't try to explain it. He said if he had a coat of arms, that would be its motto.

You could not force an excitable mind into a calm mold. Ivy knew, because she kept trying. Frank's way of looking at things seemed so *simple,* an attitude anyone, with application, could imitate. She seethed, trying to match his composure.

He'd taken to carrying his lunch in a brown bag to school. "Cheaper," he said, in the hearing of everyone in the cafeteria when one of the boys asked about it.

Carrie Gibson, of Madge's bunch, had looked with raised brows at Ivy, who gave a light, trembly laugh and said, "Oh, Francis is the miser of the family."

"*I* see," said Carrie. Clearly, so did everyone else. Did that bother or embarrass or *wound* Frank? Like heck it did.

Again and again Ivy would decide her brother had no feelings to be touched, and repeatedly he'd prove her wrong.

One chilly, foggy morning they were walking

toward the El when Ivy spied, across the street, an old man fumbling through the contents of a garbage pail, turning things over with shaking hands. It was not an unusual city sight, but it was one that made Ivy feel ripped apart with sadness and anger.

"I can't *bear* that," she cried. "Why do people get born if this is what they come to, any of them?"

What did God, who was looking at everybody all the time, *say* to Himself when He saw that? Didn't He care? He was *supposed* to care. So why did He let things happen like that?

"Bear what?" said Francis. He and Megan were walking along talking, as if what they had to say *mattered* while old men searched through garbage for something to eat.

"Don't you even *see* that? Doesn't anything matter to you?"

"That old guy? Yeah, I saw. What am I supposed to do?"

"Care! Feel about somebody besides yourself!"

Frank looked at her thoughtfully, then crossed the street and walked back to the man, his sisters trailing nervously.

"Sir," he said, holding out his lunch bag. "Would you like to have this?"

With a blear-eyed, astonished gaze, the old man squinted at the boy, at the bag. A few seconds passed, and then he said, "Grub?"

"Yup."

"What about you?"

"I can do without."

The man nodded, maybe half a dozen times, before putting out his hand to take the bag. He shambled away, turned after a few steps, and said, "Nice kid."

"Okay," said Francis, and, to his sisters, "Let's go."

Ivy knew she'd remember it all her life—that he thought of doing it, did it, and didn't think anything of having done it.

Francis of Assisi, she said to herself and was, for the moment, quite serious.

In time she made the assault on Castle Holland each morning with more confidence, though never with pleasure. Afternoons she went home almost able to forget it until time for the next day's foray. That, at any rate, was progress.

One day when they got home, Mama handed her a letter. "This came for you."

Ivy looked at the envelope, at her mother. Connie? After all this time? Not possible. Connie didn't have elegant handwriting or pale blue writing paper. The one time she had sent a card, ages ago, of the unicorn tapestries at the Cloisters, she'd used a pencil, not a pen with blue ink.

Mrs. Larkin stood by, smiling. As if, Ivy thought, making one of her occasional steps toward closeness with her mother, as if she knows that something like this has to be approached slowly. You wouldn't use up a letter all at once, as if it were a thing you got every day.

She turned the envelope around. Isabel Lerner, with an address in Brooklyn. Miss Lerner from the library had written to her!

She gave her mother a bright, embracing glance, the messenger rewarded. "It's from Miss Lerner at the library. I mean, she used to be at—" She sighed. Words escaped her.

"I knew it would make you happy."

"Oh, yes. It does. I think I'll read it in my room."

"Of course."

Opening the envelope with careful fingers, so that the flap came away without tearing, Ivy unfolded the single blue sheet.

Dear Ivy,

This is a tardy note to say I was sorry to leave our library—yours and mine—without having a chance to say good-bye. I am working in Brooklyn now, closer to my home. I wanted to tell you that I miss your pleasant presence. So far, no one with your special joy in reading has come into this branch, but one can always hope. Maybe one day our paths will cross again. Meanwhile, I don't have to tell you to keep reading. Might as well say keep breathing, eh? But I wonder, have you tried *Jane Eyre* yet? It's a beautiful book. Too old for some people your age, but not, I am sure, for you. Thank you for the many bright and happy moments you gave me.

Affectionately,
I. L.

Ivy read it three times, and a fourth. Then she put it back in the envelope and placed it in *The Harp-Weaver.*

Affectionately, I. L.

We have the same initials, Ivy thought, taking it for a sign.

Affectionately! The many bright and happy moments you gave me! Oh, it was so wonderful, so very wonderful. . . .

From her drawer in the dresser she got a box of notepaper (pink! Why hadn't she thought to buy blue?) that she'd provided herself with in order to write to Connie and Trixie and Anne, something she had not done *yet.* She pushed her pillows against the wall and settled to write a nice long reply. She supposed it wasn't the thing to do—answer a letter as soon as you got it. Maybe after she'd written it, she should put it away for a few days before sending it.

But she wanted to answer now, while all the things she wished to say tumbled in her mind. *I miss you, I miss you,* she wanted to tell Miss Lerner. *The library is so different without you, and Mrs. Hargreaves—* No. Better not criticize Mrs. Hargreaves. Just—*The library isn't the same without you.* She would say that

135

she'd get *Jane Eyre* right away. She had already read it, but she wanted to make Miss Lerner feel that her suggestion was very good, and if she admitted that she'd read it *before* the suggestion—

"Oh, dear," she said to Pickwick, who glanced up from his place on Megan's bed, where he was waiting, waiting. "I don't really know what to say, except dear dear dear Miss Lerner . . . I miss you." How could she make a letter out of that?

"Dear Miss Lerner," she wrote. "It was so nice"— she erased the adjective—"so wonderful to get your letter. The library is not the same—"

It took her nearly an hour to write two and a half pages of remarks that, in the end, came to the same thing—*dear Miss Lerner, I miss you.* . . .

PART FOUR

SIXTEEN

In november, Franklin Delano Roosevelt was elected president of the United States, and Mr. Larkin lost his job.

Ivy, Francis, and Megan came in from school on a rainy, windy afternoon shortly before Thanksgiving to find their parents in the living room, staring at each other in a silence flooded with undercurrents. They did not have to be told that something awful had happened. They walked in, looked at their mother and father, and they knew.

They remained in the hallway, Megan with her arms wrapped around her books, hands shoved in her coat sleeves (she'd lost her gloves again); Frank, about to scratch his left calf with his right foot, arrested on one leg, like a stork; Ivy shivering still from the winter wind and now from a far greater sense of cold here in their apartment.

"I *said* I have been canned." Mr. Larkin spoke in a

slow, harsh tone. "Plain English. You want it in Irish?"

Their mother was on the sofa, holding her arms tight against her body, face pale, lips tight. She looked at her husband without blinking. He leaned against the table, hands in his pockets, eyes on the floor. It was so quiet that they could hear the alarm clock in their bedroom pecking at time.

"Didn't they say anything about when you'll be called back? I mean, they can't run the Department of Transportation without men, and you're one of their best—"

"They did not say a blessed thing. They *said* no word atall. The pink slip was in me envelope, and the pink slip says it all. A scorpion doesn't *explain* that it's going to sting. No need in these cases for the sound of a human voice, the touch of a human hand."

"Oh, who cares anyway? You'll get another job, Jack. You'll get a better one. There is always room for a good electrician."

"I wonder, now, how many good electricians are out on the street this moment? How many more will there be tomorrow?" He pushed his jaw out and rubbed his neck in a strangling motion, then noticed his children, standing like statues in the hall.

Immediately, their words falling over in disorder, they began to say the soothing, covering-up things that parents say to their children in time of danger.

It was a terrible evening. For dinner they had Campbell's baked beans with frankfurters. Frankfurters at home did not have the glamour of hotdogs at Coney Island or on the Staten Island Ferry. Ivy wondered if with Pop out of work they would ever ride on the ferry again, ever take another ramble.

Would their own father have to shuffle in a bread line? Would he get a tin cup and go begging? Some apples to offer to passersby on a cold street corner? Would he stand shivering in an alley singing "The Road to Mandalay" in his deep voice and wait for coins wrapped in newspaper to be pitched down to him? She wondered if Pop, her *father*, would walk up one day to some man on the street who looked like a *working* man and silently ask for a handout? What did people do whose father got *canned*?

Mr. and Mrs. Larkin didn't eat much. They drank a lot of coffee. The children ate, in spite of the silence, but afterward Megan had to throw up.

"Now, see here," Mama said, when she and Megan had come out of the bathroom. "Look. This will not do. I still have my job, you know. That will tide us over until your father finds another one. We'll just have to tighten our belts. It is ridiculous for us to stop talking, and get sick, and be frightened this way when we *know* your father will get another job right away. We must not panic."

She ran across the room and put her arms around her husband's head, holding it close to her heart. "It is awful. Awful, awful, awful! Such a wonderful man, who knows so many things, to be fired from a stupid job that isn't worthy of him. Oh, you should have been able to finish college. Jack, you *should* have. It's all wrong that you couldn't finish. And it was my fault." She began to cry, and Megan put her head down and sobbed softly.

Francis and Ivy exchanged looks. He isn't going to say it, she thought. But I will. "Mama! Mama, we do *not* have to go to that school. It's too expen—"

Mrs. Larkin's head jerked up. She wiped her eyes with her knuckles. "Ivy, don't you dare! Don't let me hear this kind of talk again. Somebody in this family is going to get a decent education, and you children are going to that school while I have a breath left in me. Maybe I can work a double shift. I could probably get private duty at night right there in the hospital. That would mean," she continued, frowning in concentration, "that I'd better switch to the three-to-eleven shift and go right on from eleven to seven. And in *that* case, you three will have to be sensible, self-reliant, grown-up children, and when you get home in the afternoon you'll look after Megan and see to dinner. I'll write out lists for you. Groceries to get, chores to do—"

"Maybe," her husband interrupted, "you could work a triple shift, so I could go back to college."

Ivy laughed nervously, and Francis sent a wild look around, seeking the exit.

"My job, Moira, isn't—wasn't—stupid," Pop went on. "I liked it. In a way. Anyway, I *had* it, and it was not a stupid man's job."

"That was not what I meant!" she cried out. "Don't take things and twist them—"

Pop didn't like that job much when he had it, Ivy

142

thought. But anyone could see that losing a job would make it seem a good one.

"Are you just going to give up this way?" Mrs. Larkin asked. "Putting everything in the past tense, when you've been out of work one day?"

"Francis Bacon now, that wily slippery British genius—he said plenty of good stuff," Mr. Larkin continued, almost dreamily. " 'He that hath wife and children hath given hostages to fortune.' He said that. Sometimes I think a man then spends his life getting up the ransom."

"Meaning exactly what? The price of wife and children is too high for you all of a sudden?"

"I didn't say that atall, atall. I was after making a litr'y observation. Jaysus, can't a man—"

"Stop that! Stop it! I don't want to hear your stage mick representations. I want you to act like a man! And did Francis Bacon, *by* any chance, stop to think that women give more hostages to fortune than any man ever dreams of doing?"

"Then I'm acting like a man, so. Can't have it both ways."

"What are they talking about?" Francis whispered to Ivy. "What's all that mean?"

Ivy, in a moment of insight, said, "They're trying to—to *wound* each other."

"Great. Just dandy. Do you know why, maybe?"

"Because they're hurt, I suppose."

"Swell. Where does that leave us?"

"Nowhere different, I guess. After a while they'll say they're sorry."

"Children," said Mama, "why don't you go into your room and read or something. Do your homework. And don't worry yourselves sick. We'll work this out."

"Where's this morning's paper?" Pop asked roughly. "Don't bother, I've got it. Where's the damned employment section?" He shook the paper out. His hands, too, shook. He stayed with the paper until his children had left the room.

In the bedroom, Francis tried to pace. Being nervous made him restless. There wasn't enough room to pace, so he sat on his bed and pushed his fists against his face. "Well, he will get another job," he said to Ivy. When she didn't answer, he turned to Megan. "Don't worry," he told her. "He'll have a job in no time."

Megan finished putting Edward into his pajamas and said, "I'm taking Pickwick for his walk."

"Want me to come along?" Francis asked.

"No, thank you. He wants to be alone with me."

Meaning she wants to be alone with him, Ivy thought. Megan's face was still streaky with tears, but she'd retreated to her animal world, where human disasters were unrecognized.

After she'd gone, Frank got out his math books and looked around, scowling. "I don't like doing homework on my bed. It's not comfortable."

Usually they did it on the living room table, scene not only of meals but also of jigsaw puzzles, paper valentine creating, Parcheesi and dominoes and bridge. Obviously Frank did not want to go into the living room with his parents. Neither did Ivy.

"The hell with homework," she said.

"Oh, I can see this's gonna be great. Round one of the Larkin free-for-all. Sometimes, when bad times befall a family, they get nicer to each other. But not us, oh boy. We're gonna be the kind that—" He gave some thought to what kind he meant, then said unexpectedly, "Like the gingham dog and the calico cat that side by side on the table sat—we'll eat each other up. . . ."

Ivy lay back on her bed and closed her eyes.

During the first couple of weeks, when their father got in at night, Frank would say, "Any luck, Pop?" He stopped doing that.

Their mother was able to get her floor hours switched to three to eleven, and she got a private duty case right away that took from eleven at night to seven in the morning.

"I don't see how people can afford to be sick at all," Pop said. "Let alone with luxuries like private rooms and beautiful nurses. Wouldn't mind being sick myself."

"Not everyone is poor. I suppose we should be thankful."

"Mama," Frank asked one day, when she was having a cup of tea before going to her bed until noon. "This is going to be too hard for you, isn't it? I mean, how can you keep working like this with just about no sleep, and—"

"Don't worry about it, Frank. I'll be fine until your father finds work. Actually, there are several nurses at the hospital doing double shifts. It's not so bad. I don't think I could do a double floor shift, but this way I get to snooze in a comfortable chair, and old Mr. Waterhouse is such a nice man. Very considerate. Some patients can be tyrants. Don't fuss, honey. I'm fine. Fussing makes me nervous." She leaned over and held his hand briefly. "You understand?"

"I guess," Francis mumbled.

They didn't eat each other up. After his rage on that first night, a fury directed everywhere, so really nowhere, Pop settled into a grimly calm job-hunt. He was out in the weather all day. In her thoughts, Ivy followed him as he trudged in worn shoes from place to place, coat collar turned up, hands in his pockets. She fixed him a sandwich each morning, and he said he stopped to have a cup of coffee with it. She hoped he was telling the truth.

They came out of the building in the morning to a bitter littered wind, or a frigid stillness, and walked with their heads down, not speaking, their breath making ice clouds on the air. The days were cold and sunless now. The metal stairway leading up to the El platform rang hollowly, and although there was a beautiful black coal stove glowing inside the station shed, there were always so many people already in there that they usually found themselves out on the platform, shivering as they waited for their train.

After school, Frank changed into old clothes and went to the public school yard to play handball.

"How can you do that?" Ivy asked. "It's so ghastly cold out."

"It's warm in?"

"The radiators work, at least."

"You don't get the point sometimes, do you?"

She got it, but somehow misery seemed easier to bear next to a radiator.

"Frank doesn't like to stay home much," Megan said.

"No."

"I hope he doesn't catch cold." When Ivy didn't reply, she went on, "Do you think Valentino's ears get cold, sticking out of his hat?"

These days Valentino was wearing a felt hat with a wide brim. He had a heavy blanket over his bony back. Mr. Perine took good care of his old horse. Still, there were the ears, out in icy air.

"Probably not," said Ivy. "His ears are covered with fur, after all."

There was the sound of the key in the lock, and Pop came in. For a moment he stood in the small hallway to absorb the comfort of moist warmth issuing from steam radiators. He took off his thin wool gloves and rubbed his hands together, then came into the living room and dropped into his chair, still with his coat on, and smiled at them. Ivy could see it was

147

not the smile of success. Not the smile of a knight who'd gone forth and skewered the dragon, or the smile of a man who'd gone forth and speared a job, which would be the harder task.

A kind smile, a brave smile, given because he loved them. That sort of smile.

SEVENTEEN

AT THANKSGIVING, the students of Holland were asked to bring something to put in baskets that were then distributed to the poor. Mrs. Larkin managed to give each of her children an offering. A package of walnuts for Megan, a bag of cookies for Ivy, a can of pumpkin for Francis.

The stage in the Assembly Room was like a grocery store, with pupils trooping in and out, most of them with *bags* full of benefactions. For the poor, Ivy said to herself, which, then, did not include the Larkins? Cheeks dusky, she hurried onto the stage, put down her cookies, and fled.

You did this to me! she yelled at her mother out of the pit of her humiliation. You did this! Betrayed us. Shamed me. I hate you. I wish you'd *die!*

When she got home that afternoon, she found her mother on hands and knees, scrubbing the kitchen floor. Singing in her high, sweet, sort of crackling voice.

Always, always working, Ivy thought. Does she ever do anything but work? Why does she sing?

"Mama, I love you!" Ivy said fiercely.

"Goodness," said her mother, sitting back on her heels. "I love you, too. So it comes out even. That's nice."

"Mama—"

"And you are getting to—to like the school better, aren't you?"

Ivy's teeth clamped together.

"Ivy, I have such plans, such dreams." Mrs. Larkin got to her feet, emptied the bucket in the sink, and wrung out the sponge. "Things are going to be different for you children."

"Different from what?"

"Ivy! From what we've had, your father and I. Work, work, work. No education, no"—she spread her arms—"wide world to conquer!" Still Ivy said nothing, and her mother went on. "College! You are *all* going to go to college. Right through the whole four years."

"Suppose we—suppose I don't want to?"

"You must want to. Why do you think I work the way I do, why do we all go without, and make do, and—"

"I don't know why."

"When the time comes, you'll want to go."

"Maybe. Probably. I could go to college from a public school." She watched as her mother made fists of her reddened hands and shook them in the air before her face.

"Look, Ivy. Listen to me. You don't seem to understand what I'm saying. I suppose you could get in someplace like—oh, NYU or City College. But The Holland School sends its girls to the Seven Sisters!"

"There's no place better than Hunter."

"I'll have you know that your beloved poetess went to *Vassar*. Wouldn't you like to go where she went?"

"Poet."

"What?"

"Edna Millay is a poet. Poetesses write little verses for ladies' magazines."

The light and the fervor faded from her mother's face. "So hoity-toity. So hard." She turned away, began listlessly to take the supper things from the icebox, and turned again. "I think you just don't have the guts to stay at Holland. Because everything about it isn't exactly to your taste. That's what I think."

"Bless me, Father, for I have sinned."

"I'm listening, my child."

Turning her head from side to side, wishing she had the courage to bolt, Ivy faced the little grille through which she could just see the hand of the priest shading his eyes. She knew it was Father Cusick, but did he know it was she? How could he, all the children he had to listen to? She could just open the door of the confessional and run. No, she could not.

"I'm waiting, my daughter."

151

"But you see, this is my—this is the worst—" She sighed. "I can't."

"You must. If you feel that what you have done is mortal—"

"I don't know if it is. It's just—horrible."

"Then you must confess, or you will have no absolution and no peace. Go on. I'm listening."

Ivy burst out, "I wished that my mother would die, and I meant it!"

"You meant it when you wished it."

"Yes!" She began to cry.

"Why did you have this wish?"

"Oh, gee . . ." She pulled a handkerchief from her pocket, blew her nose, pushed her hair back, and found it sweaty. It was too close in here. Maybe she was going to faint?

"I'm waiting, my child. Do you know what caused you to have this wish?"

Ivy whimpered. She would have to tell him, because if she didn't, she wouldn't be absolved, and that she could not stand. To kill her mother, just so she wouldn't have to go to school! She must be washed clean of that. Pop would never force them to continue there if they didn't want to, so if Mama *were* to—

"Oh, God!" she cried out, forgetting Father Cusick.

"He is here," said the priest, and waited.

"Well. Oh, gosh . . . well, it's this *school* Mama makes us go to. This private school. We—I—don't want to go there, I can't stand it there even if what can't be cured must be endured like my aunt always

152

says. Why should I endure something because my
mother's a snob, well, not exactly a snob, but she has
these ideas about— Look, I can*not* make her understand how I—" The cat was out of the bag now. Father Cusick, who knew everything about his parish,
would know which children were going to a private
school uptown that the family could not afford to send
them to. He'd also know that the father of this family, without in any way explaining, would not allow
his children to attend the local parochial school. Yes,
Father Cusick would have her spotted now.

"Do you dislike the school altogether, or are there
times, aspects, that please you in any way?" the priest
asked.

Ivy settled back a little. "It's a *nice* place, the
building, I mean. Really beautiful. The teachers are
good, except I don't like them and they don't like
me." She waited for comment and thought she de-
tected an unspoken one. "Well, the art teacher. And
Mr. McClellan, who teaches Latin. I guess they like
me all right. Maybe. But none of the other kids do.
My brother says it's something wrong with *my* attitude, but they're just a bunch of snobs." She stopped,
breathless.

"An entire school of nothing but snobs?" said Father Cusick.

"Yes," Ivy said stubbornly. She blew her nose again
and added forlornly, "None of that is a good reason
for—for— Oh, it's so terrible, what I wished!"

"Not so terrible. My child, at your age you must
accept the discipline of the grownups in your life.

153

Parents, teachers, the clergy, even chance-met adults are in a position to impose their will on yours, and this is, on the whole, good. By virtue of having lived longer and caring very much that you grow up properly, they guide you. But it's frustrating for you. It is quite natural that the young should resent guidance, and natural to rebel. But since rebellion is only possible in the mind, children permit themselves any extreme, knowing nothing will come of it. Now, it is *not* good to clear your mother out of your path by killing her in your mind, but you know and I know that you did not mean it, even if you thought you did."

"No," Ivy whispered. "I didn't. I did, but not really."

"Now, go. Say ten Hail Marys and ten Our Fathers and make a good act of contrition. And come back next week."

"Thank you, Father."

"Bless you, my child."

As was always the case on holidays, Aunty arrived early on Thanksgiving morning to do the cooking, and Mama was happy to hand over the job, acting in the role of potboy herself.

"You know what I think," said Frank. "I think Mama would like to put nosebags on us, like Valentino's. Raw oats. That way she wouldn't have to cook at all."

"Stop criticizing Mama!" Ivy snapped.

"That's not a criticism. It's an observation." He shrugged. "Anyway, I don't mind. I *like* canned beans, and hash with an egg on it, and all that other junk. Suits me fine."

He meant it. Frank just wanted to keep his stomach filled, and canned hash and raw vegetables and apples filled it well enough. He positively loved peanut butter and claimed he'd be happy to live on it.

Just the same, Aunty's arrival with nuts to shell, and olives, and celery stuffed with cheese, and sweet potatoes that she would boil and then put in the oven with marshmallows on top, and the makings of pies, and—oh, wonderful, wonderful—a huge turkey that would take almost all day to roast, filling the apartment with *ambrosial* odors—that was a mouthwatering, peerless, and incomparable joy. When Ivy said this to Frank, he frowned and then laughed. "I guess you've got more adjectives than a dog has fleas."

"Do you think—do you think that just once, for a complete and entire *change*, you could say something nice to me? I mean, you might find it *interesting*, like uncharted territory. . . ."

"Oh, heck, Ivy. I didn't mean anything. I mean, it's kind of interesting, your vocabillary."

"Gee, thanks. I'll live on that for a week or two."

"Come to think of it, you don't exactly sprinkle me with graciosity."

"Where do you get those stupid *words*?"

"Right in my head here."

"Well, you shouldn't let them loose. They might infect somebody."

Frank turned away, and she said quickly, "I'm sorry.

I know I sound awful, but I've got this awful feeling—"

"What awful feeling?" he asked warily. "Haven't we got enough awful feelings without you thinking up more?"

"It's just—what do you think Pop's going to say when he gets home and finds Aunty and Unk have brought the Thanksgiving dinner after he said he wasn't going to eat the light or the dark meat of charity? He *said* no turkey."

"Crimers. Did you have to remind me? Boy, can you ever take the joy out of things. Ivy! For Pete's sake don't start crying! I mean, cut it out, will you?"

"Why should Ivy be after crying, pray?" said their father at the door of their bedroom. "What would the occasion be for tears, when the household is stuffed to the rafters with festive odors and provender?"

"Pop!" Frank wailed. "What are you going to do?"

"Be aisy, son, be aisy. I'll not deprive the rest of you of this bounty. I simply plan not to partake meself."

Now Ivy did begin to cry. "Oh, it's terrible. This feeling is terrible!" She took a deep breath. "If you won't eat, neither will I," she said to her father.

He closed his eyes, folded his lips in, took hold of the back of his neck as if to hold his head on. "So that's the way of it, is it? All right. I'll eat. I'll even be gracious and thankful. Will that suit, Ivy?"

She said yes, but it didn't. The beautifully cooked dinner was eaten—not in silence, but in sadness.

EIGHTEEN

THE SATURDAY BEFORE the Christmas holidays began, Ivy said to her mother, "Could we not go to school next week, please?"

"And why not, pray?"

"Mama. Because. They want us all to bring a present again. For poor people. Like at Thanksgiving."

Mrs. Larkin's mouth thinned. For a moment she didn't reply, and then burst out, "Isn't there anyone else in that place on scholarship? Are we the *only* ones?"

"No. But nobody else is . . ."

"Go on, go on. Nobody else is what?"

It was not like her mother, forcing a person to say what they both knew and anyway didn't want to admit.

"Nobody else is *poor*. Not the way we are. Not that I can see." Nobody besides us, she thought, ought to be getting, not giving, free presents at Christmas.

"Do they make you feel it there? *Feel* poor? The other children?"

Mama, you're unbelievable. You ask that *now?* You should have asked it months ago.

"I'll find something," Mrs. Larkin said.

"Find something?"

"For your *presents*, Ivy. For you three to take to school. When they're all wrapped up, no one will—"

"Isn't that cheating? Some kid gets a wrapped-up present and thinks maybe there'll be something marvelous in it. Maybe that's the only present they get, those kids. So the one from me will get five balloons and some bird cards from the baking soda box, or something like that?"

Mrs. Larkin put her hand to her forehead, as if against actual pain. "I'll get you something adequate. More than adequate. And you are going to school next week, understand? They won't defeat us. We'll—hold up our heads." She lifted her chin.

Peachy, thought Ivy, wishing she could say, "You go hold yours up at Holland and I'll hold mine up in the bedroom."

Her mother went to the hall closet, got out her coat, and yanked it on.

"Where are you going?"

"Out."

"Can I come, too?"

"No."

She returned in a couple of hours, lingered in the hall a moment putting away her coat, then came into the living room and said, "Come with me, Ivy. No, not you, Megan. Jack, I'm glad you got here. Play cards with Megan or read to her. Come on, Ivy."

"You're going to hide Christmas presents from me!" Megan said, eyeing her mother's shopping bag. Other years, much had been made of packages smuggled in, concealed, wrapped at night when the children were in bed. Ivy had noticed no preparations for Christmas this year. No presents that she knew of. No talk of when to get the tree from the man who sold them in a lot on Canal Street. No move to get down the ornaments stored on the top shelf of the hall closet between one year and the next. No popcorn chains begun. No . . . well, no anything. She could not believe that Christmas would come and *nothing* be done. But what? When? Time was getting short.

Her mother sat on Frank's bed with the shopping bag. "Now, you'll see. This year you won't have to be ashamed of your gifts at that school. It's almost a pity to wrap them. I'd like those other people to see. I'd like to show *them*."

Clearly, Mama was coming to resent the school. Calling it "that place." Showing *them*. Why, why, why would a person oblige her children to go to a school where it was necessary to *show them?*

"Mama, please. *Please* let me ask. *Why* should we—"

"Enough! No more!

"But—"

"Ivy!!"

159

"I'm only saying," Ivy yelled, "that it doesn't make sense!"

"It makes sense to me, and as long as I'm earning the money around here, people are going to do as I say."

Ivy turned her head away. "I hope Pop didn't hear you."

"Ivy Larkin, don't you *dare*. Don't you make me sound as if I'm saying something—something heartless and unkind. You misinterpret. You deliberately misinterpret. What I said has nothing to *do* with your father. But where school is concerned, you children will do as I say."

"You're earning the money," Ivy muttered under her breath. If she heard, Mama pretended not to.

"You know, Ivy, I've done this for *you*. You could at least look at these things."

Talk about twisting meanings. Did it for *me?* Mama, you make me laugh, and that's all about it.

She turned and fixed her eyes on the three objects her mother had put on the bed.

"Now this," said Mama, holding up a little gray felt Eeyore, adorably exactly like Eeyore in the books, his head down, his tail just the right tail, "is for Megan."

"Oh, Mama! Mama, she's going to love it!"

"Are you deliberately trying to drive me crazy? It's for Megan to *give*. At the school. It is a highly suitable present, and these others"—she gestured at a copy of Hans Christian Andersen with lovely illustrations and a set of Chinese checkers—"are for you and Francis to take. This year, you needn't be ashamed of your presents for the *poor*." She rummaged in the shopping bag. "I have tissue paper and seals. And ribbon." All at once she slumped, hands in her lap. "I pawned the ring to get these things, Ivy. So you go to school next week, and you'll have nothing to be ashamed of."

She isn't, Ivy thought, a person who gets defeated. She finds a way to get her way. Years ago, Mr. Larkin had won a hundred dollars in the Irish Sweepstakes. He had spent it on a wide gold wedding band with emeralds in it for Mama. Everyone, including, Ivy supposed, her mother, thought he was crazy. But all admitted it was a grand gesture. The ring had been hocked before, but not for the purpose of buying things for poor kids so that the Larkin kids could go to school with their heads up.

Ivy stood. "I'm going to the library."

"You won't help me wrap these—"

"No. I won't."

She walked too fast to notice the cold. Inside the library it was warm and smelled of pine boughs. Mrs. Hargreaves had put Christmas greens on top of the shelves. She had a bunch of holly with red berries on her desk and a pin shaped like a Christmas tree, green and red glass, on her sweater. She looked up as Ivy came to return *The Scarlet Letter*.

"Do let me, for your own good, dear, suggest a

slightly different program of reading. You see, if you read books now that are too old for you, books that you just cannot get the meaning of yet, the chances are you will not go back to them in later years, and so they'll be lost to you forever. Which would be a pity, wouldn't it?"

"Miss Lerner says rereading has been almost more important to her than reading something in the first place. Miss Lerner says she rereads some books lots of times, and every time she gets more meaning out of them. She says that if you read books when you're young, then you are *more* likely to go back to them in later years. That's what she says."

"Well. Well, we must not dispute the pronouncements of Miss Lerner. Far be it from me—"

In an attempt to propitiate, Ivy said, "But I do thank you. I mean, for trying to help me."

"Perfectly all right," said the librarian, looking at some papers at her desk.

Ivy wanted to say that *The Scarlet Letter* had been sort of over her head. Not altogether. There was something concealed in there that she'd missed. One day she'd go back and search for it. But this time she'd even skipped some. No use now to tell Mrs. Hargreaves, who had turned to a man returning a bunch of westerns.

Upstairs, she went through the deserted stacks to a chair by a window at the farthest end and huddled there, allowing the misery she'd held in check till now to flood over her. She leaned forward, head on her fists, and whispered angry words to herself. "You stupid idiot, are you ever going to learn anything? You *dumbbell* . . .''

Why did she keep getting on the wrong side of people? Lacking an instinct for it, how could she find the right side?

She thought of her mother, back there alone in the bedroom with the presents that she'd hocked her wedding ring to buy, maybe just staring at the tissue paper and the ribbon, feeling abandoned. Betrayed. As I'd feel, Ivy thought, unable to comprehend a sensation if it was not one she could experience.

How could I *do* that to her—leave her by herself that way, without a word of kindness or of thanks?

She ran all the way home and rushed into her mother's arms. "I'm sorry, I'm sorry. . . . Oh, Mama, I am so awfully *sorry!*"

"Hush. Hush, my love. It's all right. I'm sorry, too. We must be—kinder to each other."

Leaning her head against that sturdy, slender shoulder, Ivy said peacefully, "Yes. From now on. Always." She gave herself a few minutes more of the haven she found sometimes in her mother's arms, then sighed and sat up. "Where are the others?"

"Your father's gone with Megan to find us a tree—"

"We're going to have one? I'm glad. But it would've been all right if we couldn't."

"There won't be much besides a tree, I'm afraid," Mrs. Larkin said, with a little gesture of helplessness.

"Mama. It's all right. Please believe me. We don't really mind at all. Come on . . . let's wrap the presents for the poor children. . . . Where's Frank? Did he see any of this stuff? It's really awfully nice. I love the book."

"I don't know where he is. At Murphys, I guess. I heard they have bedbugs. Do you think that's true?"

"I don't know. I never go there."

"If they do, I hope Frank doesn't bring any home. Cockroaches are quite enough, thank you."

"Except Archy, of course."

"I will always make an exception for a cockroach who practices *vers libre*."

She was happy now, here with her mother, wrapping the presents that she no longer resented having to give away, being silly together like a couple of girls.

NINETEEN

The school week came to an end on Wednesday, and now they had a clear run into January before they had to think about it again.

On Thursday, the Larkin children went out together to do their Christmas shopping. There was a gusty, knife-keen wind. Ice patches mottled the sidewalk. There had been no sun for days, and they were praying it would snow before the weekend.

Francis and Ivy had been saving most of their allowance of a quarter a week for a couple of months. Megan, unable to deprive either Valentino of his licorice or her alley cats of their scraps, contributed what she had—thirty cents. Among them, they had four dollars.

"Will you put my name on the presents, too?" Megan asked.

"In very small writing," said Francis.

"Anyway," Megan said. "I've got my little dishes."
At Holland, the first grade had fashioned small clay

165

dishes to be used as pin or ashtrays. Painted, fired, and glazed, they were quite handsome. Megan had made three. One for her parents, one for Aunty and Unk, one for Aunt Anna and Uncle Jim and Aunt Tess. She had painted a scene on each, the same scene with variations, the backside of a bunny sitting under a leafless tree.

Their destination now was a secondhand store on Market Street. A dim and dusty emporium that sold books, trinkets, games, old jewelry, toys, china, and things called bric-a-brac. Francis had a habit of dropping in here to browse through the bookshelves, looking for first editions. He assured a skeptical Ivy that in this way people uncovered books worth fortunes. He'd read about a man who found a first edition of *Life on the Mississippi* in a grimy old attic bookshop, and he'd got a thousand dollars for it, or maybe ten thousand. Francis was ever on the alert for treasure. For Mrs. Perine's gold wedding band, for coins dropped on the sidewalk, for loot in a paper bag abandoned by fleeing burglars. He'd read about that, too. It had actually happened, right here in New York City.

And, in fact, he had once found a dollar bill, crumpled in the gutter near Valentino's hoof. Megan had been feeding the horse, Ivy waiting patiently beside her, reading. Frank, restless, had glanced around, looked down, and let out a yell. "Lookit! Lookit what I found!" Her sisters glanced over to see him waving a dollar in the air.

"Where did that come from?" Ivy demanded.

"Right there." Francis pointed. "Just lying there, waiting to be picked up by yours truly."

"It belongs to somebody," Ivy pointed out.

"Are you nuts? What d'ya expect me to do? Hold it up and holler, 'Anybody lost this folding stuff?' Boy, we'd be mobbed in a minute."

Mr. Perine, emerging from Sudowsky's Butcher Shop, tongs dangling in his hand, greeted them with his usual cheery roar.

"Maybe it belongs to him," Ivy whispered. "You found it right by his horse."

"You think the horse is his banker?" Francis looked at his sister angrily, then turned to Mr. Perine and said, "I just found this here dollar bill, Mr. Perine. Right there, by Valentino's foot. Ivy says maybe it's yours. Or maybe it's his," he added with a weak smile, looking at Valentino.

The iceman slapped his pockets anxiously, then grinned at Frank's expression. "Keep it, keep it," he said. "Finders keepers, losers weepers, eh, Valentino?" He gave his horse a mighty thump on the rump. "He'd only blow it on oats."

Francis had confessed to Ivy that ever since that day he'd dreamt at night about finding money. "Coins," he said. "Never bills. Lots of quarters and fifty centses. Boy, would I like to find a lot of money."

"Would you rather find it or make it?"

"Makes no never mind to me, just so I had it."

Ivy didn't think he had much chance of finding

money again. She wished her father could find a job and *make* some again. Not some day. Today. Anyway, in time for Christmas. That would be the best present.

Pop had become moody. He trudged the streets all day in the cold, in the rain or the snow, or the thin winter sunlight, so it was no wonder he came home at night exhausted and aching and cross. No one could blame him.

Francis did not find a first edition in the second-hand store. He did come across an old copy of *Leaves of Grass.* They bought that for Pop, for thirty cents. For forty-five cents they got a copy of *Alice Adams.* Mrs. Larkin said it was her favorite American novel. ("Not very highbrow of me, and a person should probably like *Moby Dick* best, or something by Nathaniel Hawthorne. But I love *Alice Adams.*") Some people would say it was silly to buy a person a book she'd already read or could get from the library. None of the Larkins would find it silly.

For Aunty and Unk they got a backgammon set in pretty good condition. That was eighty cents.

Then they bought, for their mother, a string of beads that the man said were crystal. ("Take them home and dip them in very hot water and ammonia, and they'll sparkle like diamonds.") Those came to one dollar and forty cents and were beautiful. The owner gave them a box lined with blue velvet to put them in.

"Boy, I can hardly wait for her to see them," said Frank.

And wasn't it true that it was almost more fun watching people get what you'd got them than getting what they'd got you?

They now had thirty-five cents each to spend on each other in the secondhand emporium. Separating for this, Ivy bought Megan's present, Megan bought Frank's, and Frank Ivy's.

A lovely afternoon's shopping.

Christmas fell on Sunday. For the first time in years, it turned out to be on Mama's weekend off. Her patient, Mr. Waterhouse, had gone home, and she put off taking another case until after the holidays.

On Christmas Eve, Mr. Larkin went out early, as usual, looking for some place that needed a good electrician. He was still trying to work at his trade. Unk said face it, electricians were a dime a dozen, and Jack should grab anything that came along. "Night watchman, soda jerk—can't be choosy, Jack," he'd said on his last visit.

When he and Aunty had gone, Pop exploded. "Oh, isn't he the grand fellow now, counseling the less fortunate?"

"Jack, don't," Mama said. "You sound bitter."

"That's not a sound, mavourneen. That's a condition. I am bitter. I feel old and cold and unemployed, and I don't need helpful hints to paupers. One other thing, while I'm about it. I don't want them bringing another turkey. If they want to eat with us on Christmas, they'll eat what we provide. Sardine sandwiches, like as not."

That conversation took place before Mrs. Larkin pawned the ring. Now she planned on Irish stew.

Their father was gone by the time Mr. Perine, on the morning of Christmas Eve, arrived with a fifty-pound block of ice on his shoulder and a turkey dangling from his left hand.

"Good morning, Mr. Perine," said Mrs. Larkin, trying not to look at the turkey. "Merry Christmas." She couldn't help it. She stared.

"Merry Christmas, everybody," he said, heaving the ice into its compartment and patting their handsome icebox in the same way he patted Valentino's rump. "Look here, Mrs. Larkin, could you folks use this turkey? Sudowsky the butcher give it to me just now. A Christmas gesture, I suppose. But the thing is, my wife already bought one over in Jersey the size of a Great Dane. For just the two of us. We'll be eating turkey until the Fourth of July. So I thought to myself, maybe Mrs. Larkin can take it off my hands—"

Mama, not demonstrative with anyone but her family, surprised her children by leaning forward and kissing the iceman's cheek. "You are a dear man. I'll be—we'll be happy to take it off your hands."

"Well—I'll just shove him in the box here and be off."

"Children, thank Mr. Perine."

Ivy, thanking him, pleased at having a turkey instead of sardine sandwiches or even Irish stew,
nevertheless felt apprehensive at the thought of what
her father was going to say. If he wouldn't take a
turkey from Aunty, would he be more agreeable about
one from Mr. Perine?

"Now, you are not to leave before you have a cup
of coffee and a bun," Mrs. Larkin said to him.

"Well. Okay. Don't mind if I do." He took off his
heavy woolen jacket, hung it carefully on the back of
the chair that he then drew up to the table. "*Say*—
that's one beautiful tree you got there."

The children looked with pleasure at the small tree
that stood on white tissue paper, representing snow,
in a corner of the room. Like the fir tree in the fairy
tale, it was splendid beyond all words. They had
made, during the evening of the past week, long chains
of colored paper loops. They had cut out cardboard
stars and gingerbread men, and strung a popcorn
chain that circled the tree from its spindly top where
the star was, to its nice wide bottom branches. They'd
hung tinsel and ornaments from the box at the back
of the hall closet shelf. The tinsel was tarnished, but
Ivy felt that made it look gold. Mama had bought a
box of silver icicles to drape here and there. She had
got some walnuts and a little bottle of gilt paint, and
Pop had carefully drilled a hole in each nut, so that
now eighteen tiny golden globes hung in the branches.
A string of colored lights—green, red, yellow, blue—
was arranged on the front branches. There were extra bulbs for when one went out, which made them

171

all go out. When this happened, Pop had to test each light in turn to get them all shining again. Other years he had done this with great patience, saying it was a necessary part of the rites of Christmas and that he, fine electrician that he was, was the very man for the job. Ivy hoped they wouldn't go out this year, or at least not until after tomorrow. The scent, the heady woodsy scent of the fir boughs, filled the air. On the radio, carols were playing softly.

Looking at their bedizened tree, Ivy realized with deep pleasure that she envied no one anywhere in the world.

She and Francis and Megan had taken their prettily wrapped presents to school on Monday, and on Wednesday morning Ivy had presented her teacher, Mrs. Charles, with a box in which was a handkerchief she'd bought at the ten-cent store. It was sort of stiff, but had a little holly leaf and berry embroidered in one corner. All the students brought presents to the teacher, and she smiled at them and said she was going to take them home to put under her tree. Relieved that there was to be no public exposure, Ivy had thought she was really a nice person. Kind. That Ivy was like her father, not wanting people to be kind to her in such a way that she had to feel grateful, was not Mrs. Charles's fault.

In the Assembly Room, there had been a tall, tremendously decorated tree, at the foot of which the

presents for the poor were piled. Every morning during that short week, the entire school had assembled
to sing Christmas songs. On Wednesday there had
been a Nativity play, given by pupils from the upper
and lower schools together. At this performance, Faye
Cameron sang a song while the three kings crossed
the stage to lay their gifts beside the cradle, where
Mary, Joseph, shepherds and angels, and humble
beasts were gathered around the Babe.

> *"We three kings of Orient are,*
> *Bearing gifts we travel afar.*
> *Moor and mountain,*
> *Field and fountain,*
> *Following yonder star. . . ."*

Faye had a clear soprano untouched by any mis-
givings about its quality. Ivy, too self-conscious even
to speak up easily in class, listened and marveled and
felt the old lump of envy that seemed to lodge just
under her ribs. Faye was slender and blond and taller
than any boy in the class. She was thirteen years old,
and you could already see what she was going to be
like at eighteen. "Some sort of *perfect,*" Ivy had muttered to herself.

But today she didn't care about Faye or anyone
else in The Holland School. She was home, and happy,
and not envious.

The afternoon was peaceful. No snow fell, but the

fragrance of the Christmas tree filled the apartment, the steam radiators chirruped like crickets, and Ivy lay on her bed reading Dickens. She loved his Christmas stories and wished she could read them to Megan, but there were too many scary, even sad parts. She was not going to jiggle her sister's new-found, puppy-found sense of security.

Just the same, if you couldn't have real snow, the next best thing was to read about snow in Dickens. *A Christmas Carol. The Holly-Tree Inn.*

Pickwick, who'd been banished from the kitchen, lay beside her. Mama and Megan were in the kitchen making cranberry relish, something Megan had learned to do at school.

So Christmasy. So shielded from the real world.

Mr. Larkin reacted to Mr. Perine's gift of the turkey as Ivy had been sure he would. He blew up.

"Throw that thing out the window, hear? Take it out and give it to some needy body you find on the street! Dump it down the dumbwaiter, but don't be trying to cook it in this house or trying to talk me into it, and that's all about it! Christmas potlatch in this house will not include charity, and that from the iceman!"

"The iceman isn't good enough to give a present?" Mama asked.

"Don't be twisting my words about! I'll not have it!"

Mama, her face quite still, gazed downward while he shouted. Then, with a slight lift of her shoulders she opened the cupboard under the sink. With fingers that fumbled (she did not ordinarily fumble), she pulled out an old brown bag, opened the icebox, reached in for the turkey, looked at it thoughtfully for a moment, and then eased it into the bag. All done slowly, slowly, while the rest of them looked on.

"Francis," she said. "Take this over to Murphys. They'll be glad of it, and we do have the stew."

"Moira!" Mr. Larkin yelled. "Put that thing back!"

She smiled and kissed him, turned to her son and said, "Then run around to your aunt's and tell her we're going to have turkey after all, so she should get here early. Unless she wants me to cook it. Say that to her."

"That'll bring her running," said Francis with a grin.

Mama put her hands to each side of Pop's face and looked into his eyes. "We do thank you, love."

"Ah—who's to make anything of it atall? Your ring in pawn, and now my honor."

"This isn't charity, Jack. It's a present from a friend. Actually, Mr. Sudowsky gave it to him, but Mrs. Perine had already got one."

"So—thank him, not me."

"I have thanked him. It was nice of him to give us the turkey, but *you* are the one who is large-spirited."

Ivy looked at them curiously. Her mother wasn't a one to offer such flaunting flattery, nor her father the man to accept it, yet it had been offered and received without a murmur. It made her uneasy.

175

Francis came back, cheeks bright and cold from his run through the wintry streets, and they sat down to Christmas Eve Irish stew.

It was Pop's turn to say the blessing, his being over in four syllables. *"Benedicte,"* he said. Ivy had asked if he didn't feel sort of a hypocrite, saying even such a short blessing, and he'd answered that he saw nothing wrong in giving thanks for food in a world where so many were hungry. "We're very lucky," he'd said, "and I'm glad to thank—somebody." That had been before he lost his job. Ivy hoped that in a way he still thought himself lucky. There was food on his table, and he had a wife and three children who all loved him very much. If that wasn't enough to make him feel lucky, she hoped that anyway it gave him comfort.

After dinner, Mama and Pop watched a play their children had written together, about animals talking to one another in stables all over the world on Christmas Eve. The message the creatures delivered in a great many words ("All our own work," Ivy emphasized in the prologue) came down to one: *Rejoice and be kind.*

It was a peculiar thing about Christmas. Even if you did not have much to rejoice about, something in the season itself urged you toward cheer.

"Christmas casts out gloom!" Ivy brayed, the donkey addressing the camel and rhinoceros, who snorted agreement. ("Rhinoceros?" Frank had protested. "Whoever heard of a rhinoceros in a stable?" "I want him there," Megan had said firmly. "He doesn't have to go right in. He can stand outside.") "No matter what befalls," Ivy the donkey continued, "the spirit of love lives on!"

She looked right at her father, who gave her as sweet a smile as ever he had in the old days, before their troubles.

When the play was over and applauded, Megan, who'd found a short piece of tinsel fallen from the tree, wound it in a circle and put it on her head, absentmindedly, not looking to see the effect on anyone, not even looking in a mirror.

She really is the youngest princess, Ivy thought. A beautiful little girl. Did Christmas cast out envy, too? Perhaps. For as long as Christmas lasted.

Then it was time for midnight Mass, and Pop went with them.

PART FIVE

TWENTY

"BLESS US, OH LORD, for these Thy gifts, which we are about to receive through Thy bounty through Christ, our Lord, amen," said Megan.

"Do you want to guess what?" said Francis the moment she'd finished. "Mrs. Murph is having another baby."

"Poor thing," said Mrs. Larkin.

"That will make how many? Fifteen?" said Mr. Larkin.

"Four. There's Johnny and Terence and Patch. Do you realize that if you have four children, your family's only twice as big as if you had only one?"

"That's not possible—" Mama began, then stopped, turning her head to puzzle it out. "My goodness, you're right. How do you know things like that?"

"Johnny and I figured it out. Does sound funny, doesn't it?" He looked at his father. " 'Smatter, Pop?"

"I'm thinking about another little Murphy let loose upon the world."

Frank grinned. "Be something, all right."

After dinner, he got up and went to the closet for his jacket. "I gotta go out for a while. Me and Johnny have a business deal to discuss."

"Johnny and I," said Mr. Larkin.

"What do you mean, business deal?" said his mother. "And take off your jacket. You aren't going anywhere at this hour."

"But, Mama—"

"Take off your jacket."

"Oh, boy." Frank threw the jacket on the floor, looked at his parents, and hunched his shoulders. "Okay, okay. I'll pick it up. I won't go anywhere at this hour."

"I knew you'd see reason," said his mother. "Now, what is this about going into business?"

"Well." Frank sat at the table again and looked earnest. "We're starting a window-washing enterprise. We're going to go around to people's apartments and offer to wash windows, ten cents apiece."

"No," said Mrs. Larkin.

"What d'ya mean, no? You're gonna be cut in on this deal. I plan on contributing half what I make to the family coffer, and that's—"

"Frank. You might as well stop talking about it because I will not permit it, and I shall certainly phone Mrs. Murphy to find out if she has any idea of what you two are—"

"That's not fair!" Francis interrupted. "Here we're showing some get-up-and-go, and you put the damper on it right away. I think that's awful. Pop!"

"Sorry. I agree with your mother. Unless you plan to wash only the insides of these windows?"

"How could you charge ten cents to wash just the insides, for Pete's sake?"

"If you're after thinking, for a *moment*, that your mother or I will allow you to sit on windowsills, hanging on with the one hand and washing a window with the other and you maybe ten floors above the street . . . well, you're mistaken. We place a certain value on you."

"But—"

"Let him go ahead and try," said Ivy. "He won't get any business. People around here wash their own windows. They don't pay to get it done." And most of them didn't do it either, she thought. It was the kind of remark that did not go down well with her parents.

"There might just be that one daft person on the seventh floor someplace who'd take him on. A risk we won't run," said Pop.

Francis still honored his father and mother to the point of not disobeying a direct order. He even, as now, often told them ahead of time something he had to know he would be forbidden to do. Ivy figured that the idea of washing windows scared him, but he hadn't wanted to say no to Johnny Murphy, so he'd said yes, knowing he'd get out of it. Frank was good at finding loopholes for himself. And he never sulked. He had Pop's tindery temper, but did not, like Pop these days, go morose for long periods.

He was always seeking ways to make money. Like

those diligent investigations of sidewalks and gutters for something of value that might have been dropped for him to find. He was also willing to work and had had several peculiar jobs already.

Like the one he'd had in Inwood. He'd hired himself out as a general helper in a grocery store for twenty-five cents a week and all the rotten produce he could carry home on Saturday evening. That had lasted a week. When, on the Saturday, he'd arrived with a big bag of soft black bananas, apples you could put your finger through, and potatoes with eight-inch eyes, Mama had dumped it down the incinerator and told him to consider himself fired.

Shortly after they'd moved here, he'd put a sign up in the lobby, offering to run cheerful errands, giving his apartment and telephone number. A few days later the sign was gone. They suspected the janitor. Frank had not put up another and hadn't been called upon to run any cheerful errands.

So it went—Frank seeking and not finding, never successful and never discouraged.

Now, the window-washing caper disposed of, he told Megan that he'd kind of like to listen to "The Shadow" if she didn't mind. She'd been lying on the floor, rereading one of her practically complete set of *Old Mother West Wind*, but got to her feet agreeably and headed for the bedroom, closely followed by Pickwick.

For a while, Ivy remained where she was. Her parents claimed to scorn the radio serials. "The Shadow," "The Lone Ranger," "The Green Hornet." Ivy had noticed that they usually listened when Frank put one on. She didn't see how they could find that stuff interesting. Probably they listened to pass the time. It seemed to her that a lot of grown-up time was just passed. Or killed.

"What do you and Aunty do when you're together?" she'd asked her mother.

"Goodness, I don't know. Kill time, I suppose. Doesn't matter, so long as we're together."

Peculiar. Working as hard as she did most of the time, her mother found it a luxury to let a few hours dribble unused through her fingers, Ivy supposed. Now she looked closely at her parents and her brother, wondering what was going on in their heads. Frank seemed really to be listening to the program. He made faces, a fist now and then, and once or twice yelped. Mama sat in her easy chair with her feet tucked under, blinking in a sleepy way. Pop had put the back of his Morris chair as far down as it would go and was just looking at the ceiling with a vacant expression.

Were they thinking? Planning? Worrying? Dreaming? Just letting time pass until they could go to bed?

"Pop," she said softly, "would you like to read something to us?"

He shook his head. "Not tonight, little lady. I'm fair done up."

"That's okay. I just thought— But it's okay."

"Hush!" said Francis. "Hush up! I'm trying to hear this!"

Ivy got to her feet and tiptoed in an exaggerated

fashion down the hall to the bedroom, where Megan was curled up with Pickwick and Edward, still reading.

"Did the program scare you?" she asked Ivy.

"Bored me."

"Most things don't scare *me* now."

"I think Frank was right. Pickwick is your lucky dog."

A pause. Then Megan, looking at her sister sideways, said, "Ivy, do you ever get afraid"—she drew a deep breath—"Do you think about somebody might *die?*"

Somebody. That means Mama or Pop, Ivy said to herself. Probably Francis or me. Or Aunt Anna. Or Aunty or Unk. She means someone in the family. Always the family, with Megan.

"Nobody will," she said resolutely.

"How do you *know?*"

"It's this feeling I have."

She did have it. Nobody in their family would die because she couldn't stand it. Mama and Pop would be—*all right.* Anyway, until we're all grown up, she thought. Look at the grandparents. On both sides— even Pop's people in Ireland that they'd never seen because they'd gone back there before Pop was even married—even they had lived till Pop was a grown person.

One day she and Megan and Francis would be grown, too. Megan would be married to a handsome man and have two children. She'd name the girl Blaise, as a favor to Ivy. Francis would be this tall, handsome fellow with a college degree. He wouldn't be a ferryboat captain or a priest, but he'd be something important.

And I? said Ivy to herself. Easy. I'll be an old maid. A spinster. As all the books informed her that unmarried ladies were obliged to become sour and dry, that's what she'd become. . . .

. "Ivy, you're staring."

"Sorry. I was thinking." I was looking at the future.

"You know what Frank says?" Megan went on. "He says that billions and billions of people have lived and then died. He says the ground must be *stuffed* with dead people."

Oh, *boy*. That Frank! Talk about talking without thinking! "That's a dumb stupid thing to say."

"He didn't say it to me." Megan was defensive for her brother. "It was when we were going in the subway where it came out of the ground on our way to Coney Island and there were all these miles and miles of graveyards. He said it to Pop, not to me."

"He should keep his stupid idea to himself."

"But I'm not afraid of a lot of things," Megan said softly, hugging her small homely dog. "Not anymore."

I could murder Frank, Ivy thought. If he and I would learn to keep our mouths shut! Things got said that should not be. Frightening, hurting, *wounding* things . . . said to people you loved and shouldn't frighten or *wound*. Saying afterward you didn't mean to didn't help.

Father Cusick said that God would always forgive people their mistakes. The hard thing, he said, was for people to forgive themselves. Only, he said, we must try, because to be unforgiving toward oneself meant eventually being unforgiving toward others, and that was a sin.

Ivy supposed he knew what he was talking about, even though she didn't entirely understand or agree. God might forgive people like Faye or Madge or Madame Gaillard their unkindness, their *hurtfulness*, but Ivy knew she would not forgive them. Nor would she try.

TWENTY-ONE

———

THERE WERE TWO PUBLICATIONS put out at The Holland School, a free-wheeling newspaper that claimed it would accept practically any submission, and a highly particular little magazine. They were staffed and produced by senior high students, each with a faculty adviser. The newspaper was *Dutch Treat*, the magazine *Delft Blue*.

In March, Ivy submitted a poem she had written to *Dutch Treat*. To send it to the magazine daunted her, but maybe there was a chance with the newspaper if they really did take just about anything.

During what seemed to her an unendurable wait to hear from the editors, she read her short and serious rhyme again and again. She did not show it to anyone in the family. Sometimes it seemed to her a good poem. Another reading would cause her cheeks to burn darkly, and she'd wonder how she could have been so puffed up with pride as to offer these lines to strange eyes.

lover & savior of man
we see you rise to the skies
and are filled with joy
but we carry the cross
the sign of our loss
since the world began

She called it "Ascension Thursday."

Leaving out punctuation had seemed to her an original touch. Now it seemed an affectation. Like e. e. cummings, a poet she loved to read and did not understand, she'd used only small letters.

A good verse? Not so bad? *Awful?* Would the editors of *Dutch Treat* take it? Laugh at it? Ignore it?

Each morning, arriving at school, she wondered if today would be the day she'd hear. The thought caused her heart to pump so that she could feel it beating in her head.

I'll never, not ever, she said to herself, do anything like this again. It isn't worth it. Nothing could be worth it.

She waited two weeks, and on a Friday morning, when she opened the lid of her desk, found an envelope lying on top of her books. It had a sepia block print in the upper left corner. *Dutch Treat.* Fancy lettering. The final *t* shaped into a windmill. *Of* course. *Ivy*, in sepia ink, was scrawled on it. Was that a good sign? Friendly? Wouldn't a rejection be addressed to Ivy Larkin, not just Ivy?

Holding the lid up, she stared for a while at the envelope, not touching it. She looked at entering stu-

dents, all busily talking or assembling books, tucked
the envelope up her sweater, and went to the girls'
room. Crowded here, too. Going into a stall, she sat
on the toilet, hesitated again, then pulled the enclo-
sure out and stabbed it with her eyes, trying to see
Yes or No in a hurry.

It was No.

She opened her mouth and pulled in a jerky breath.
Of course, No. Beneath a fickle optimism had been
this bedrock certainty of No.

Having got the message without reading it, she
tucked the sheet of paper in its envelope, slid it back
up her sweater. She might look at it later, when she
didn't feel this sick. Probably she'd just throw it out.

"You okay?" a girl asked as she emerged.

Ivy left the room, not hearing.

"That girl just doesn't *want* anyone to be friendly.
My goodness, I was just asking. She looks sort of awful, doesn't she?"

"Which girl?"

"Ivy Larkin."

"Oh. Did Andy *kiss* you last night?"

"Tried to. I ducked. I told him I don't approve of
extramarital mucking around."

"You didn't!"

"I did. I think he thought I meant I was going with
a soldier."

They went out laughing.

That evening Ivy shoved the note, still unread, beneath her bed and spent a sleepless night above it—

the sort of night when you think you haven't slept at
all and only find out you have when you wake up.

Toward noon on Saturday, with the apartment
empty—Pop job-hunting, Francis somewhere, Megan
walking Pickwick over to Aunty's, Mama at work—
she sat on the edge of her sister's bed, waiting for
her resolve to stiffen. She opened the envelope, put
aside her returned poem. Verse. She glanced first at
the signature on the letter. Victor Ryland, Ass't Editor. He was in the eleventh grade. An exhibition diver,
a gymnast. He could walk on his hands for twenty-
eight minutes and was shooting for thirty.

> Nice try, kiddo, but a bit on the spiritual side
> for our rag. Try *Blue*. By the by, the world
> didn't begin with the crucifixtion, but I ex-
> pect you're using poetic lisense. Look out for
> that, it can get you arrested, hah-hah. Try us
> again and never say die.
>
> Yrs. Victor Ryland,
> Ass't Editor.

She was sitting there, holding Edward, when her
father came in.

"Ivy?" he said. "Honey, is something wrong?"

"You're early."

"Just sick of looking, so here I am."

"It's awfully hard on you, isn't it, Pop?"

"Not what I'd choose. It'll work out." He said that
a lot. "Come on, sweetheart, what is it?"

"It isn't anything. In a way, I think it's everything. But it isn't."

"What do you mean?" he asked, sounding anxious. He sat down across from her. "What's this about? Why are you sitting here in the gloom of day all on your owny-own?"

Ivy lifted her head to meet his eyes. A sigh escaped her. "Do you think—" she began, hesitated, continued. "Do you think there's such a thing as a hard-luck person?"

"Well, you seem to think so. That's what matters. What's it about, so?"

Ivy leaned over and picked up Victor Ryland's letter, which had fallen on the floor, and handed it to him.

Mr. Larkin took it in at a glance. "You submitted something to this—this rag?" After a long pause, he said, "Tell your old man, Ivy. That's what he's here for."

"Yes." She was whispering. "A—poem."

"Would you want to show it to me, now?"

She took her verse from Megan's pillow and handed it to him.

After a moment, he looked up, leaned across the narrow space and put his hand on her twisting fingers. They grew still at his touch.

"This is a grand poem," he said. "It's *felt*." He took his hand away and laid it against his heart. "It touches me, here."

Ivy smiled at him unhappily and began to cry.

Moving over beside her, he held her close for a few minutes.

"It's okay, really," she said, groping in her pocket for a handkerchief. "I don't really care."

"Of course you care. People always care about something they've created. It's a shame, now, that this jumped-up prig, Ryland, got his dirty paws on it. Twit can't even spell."

He's so angry for me, Ivy thought. Probably she shouldn't have told him, poor Pop with his *real* problems. But his anger warmed her. Ordinarily, he'd have been amused at a high school ass't editor who couldn't spell.

"He can walk on his hands for twenty-eight minutes."

"So it takes longer than that for the blood to get to his brain."

Ivy sniffled and smiled. She was feeling better. Unexpectedly, she was feeling pretty good.

Mr. Larkin snapped his fingers. "Would you have me be laying a curse on him, now?"

"Oh, *please* do, Pop."

He made a few passes in air with his thin hands. *"May he marry a ghost who bears him a kitten, and may the High King of Glory permit him to get the mange. There. How will that do?"*

"It's a lovely curse. Thank you, Pop."

"It was nothing."

"You know, I really mean it, Pop. I don't care. I liked the writing of it, but I think it would've been sort of awful, having it there in that paper for people to see. It's too—personal."

"All poetry is personal."

"I guess. Just the same. But, Pop—now, *listen* to me, please please. That school is all wrong for me. Everything I do there seems to go wrong."

"Your—what do they call them? Not report cards—"

"Evaluations."

"Your schoolwork, according to these evaluations, is in every possible sense excellent. That's not what you're talking about, is it?"

"No." A long, tired sigh. "No. It's just that I don't fit. I started out on absolutely the wrong foot, and I've been hopping along on the same foot ever since. I wouldn't even know now where to *put* the right foot, supposing I had one. Nobody there likes me, you know."

"Now don't say that," he said, sounding alarmed. "Because I'll not believe you."

"It's true. Even if I do the work well, the teachers don't like me. Maybe it isn't that they don't like me. They don't pay attention to me. Usually teachers pay attention to people who do good work."

"Ivy. Ivy, me love. *Is* it possible that there is something about the way you're feeling toward the teachers themselves that—"

"Pop! Frank says that to me all the time. But even if it's so—I guess maybe it's so, sort of—there's nothing to *do* about it anymore. It's too late! They're too

195

used now to ignoring me, and I'm too used to hating them—"

"Hating?"

"Not liking. My other teachers liked me, in public school, because I *am* good at my work—"

"There we have the crux of it all, don't we? You never wanted to go to this school, and you've never tried to change your mind."

"Oh, let's skip it. That's the kind of thing Mama says. And Frank. Even if it's true, I don't care. I didn't want to go there, I don't want to go there, I'll never want to go there."

"Ivy, there's a thing you'd do well to understand. Your mother went from high school into nursing school. I had that year of college and quit. She feels we've been deprived of a thing of great value. Our chance to move up in the world. Moving up in the world means all the world to your mother."

"Not to you?"

"I *chose* marriage over schooling. It's not a choice I regret."

"Mama does?"

"Oh, you understand more than you're letting on, surely," he said with a touch of impatience.

"Maybe."

He got to his feet. "I'll speak to her."

"No! No, no, no! Don't *do* that! *Please?* I'll tell you something, Pop, and you have to believe me because it's true. I don't like the school, but I'm learning lots of things I'd never get to learn in public school. French and Latin. And I love the art studio. And the building—that's simply beautiful. Anybody can see that it's a lovely place to go to school in, and that should have a good effect somehow, shouldn't it? Spending most of five days a week in surroundings like that?"

Mr. Larkin looked around the small bedroom, at the homemade curtains and spreads, the orange-crate bed tables skirted in matching material.

Reading his mind, Ivy said sharply, "I like this room. Mama does everything she can to make it pretty."

He nodded. "Your point remains. It must be good for a person to spend part of the day in grand surroundings." Pop had gone to the school once, to look it over, and had never gone back, not to the Christmas play, not to the first semiannual teacher-parent talk.

"Besides," Ivy went on, "I'd go only *because* it means so much to Mama, and I won't complain anymore, honestly. It means a whole lot more to her than it doesn't mean to me. I guess that's what I'm trying to say. And I feel lots better now, telling you."

They sat for a while in silence, and then Mr. Larkin said, "What's this *Blue* he speaks of?"

"They have a magazine at the school, too. *Delft Blue.* Very snooty. Usually only upper school people get anything in it."

"I think you should try it."

"Maybe," she said. They both knew she would not. Then, speaking quickly so as not to have a chance to change her mind, she said, "Why can't I go to a parochial school?" When he didn't answer, she said stubbornly, "It isn't only Mama telling us what we have to do. You're just as—just as—"

"Would *unfair* be the word you're wanting?"

"It'd do," she said flatly. "You've never once explained. What's *wrong* with a Catholic school? It'd be a compromise, wouldn't it? Between private and public?"

She was feeling that once again he'd refuse to answer, and then he said, "Catholic schools don't let you think for yourself. They tell you what you'll believe, what you will not believe. They let their beliefs color their teaching. They dictate how you will order your life. I don't want my children pressed into *any* mold. My children are going to think for themselves."

"Then I think, for myself, I want to go to Catholic school."

They stared at each other.

"People who are going to think for themselves," Ivy went on, "*do* it. No matter where they go to school. I think you're prejudiced, that's what I think."

"Oh, do you now?"

"Yes."

"That's a pretty serious charge you're after making to the one father you've got."

"You're prejudiced and Mama's a snob." She remembered Father Cusick saying to her that young people allowed themselves any extreme in rebellion. "Pop, I don't mean that."

"Well, you do. To an extent. To an extent, you're in the right of it. How old are you, Ivy?"

"Oh, Pop! I'm nearly fifteen!"

"Only that," he said. "You sound older."

Another silence. Ivy felt that this time her father wasn't going to break it. She said, "It doesn't matter about that, either, Pop. The parochial school, I mean. I think I'm just getting around to going to school and learning and not caring about the rest."

"The rest being a bit of fun, a touch of pleasure in your days of learning?"

She shrugged.

"Oh, you are growing up. Right before me eyes, and that's the truth of the matter. Don't be going too far too fast now, will you? That'd break your old da's heart altogether."

He could always make her laugh.

"Do you ever wish," she said, straightening, "that you were someplace else, that you could be transported on a magic carpet to another part of the world entirely?"

"Everyone must, surely."

"If right this minute, *now*, you could be anywhere in the world you wanted, where would you be, Pop?"

Mr. Larkin looked at the ceiling. "If that were the case, Ivy honey, I'd stand this minute in the middle of the county of Connemara, the way I'd be only a couple of miles from Ballyconneely. I'd walk to there, with the rain falling soft as pollen on me face and the sheep bleating in the meadow and the fishermen rowing in to Slyne Head at close of day with a great catch." He smiled at her dreamily. "And where would you be?"

"With you, of course. Pop, why don't we move to Ireland since you miss it so much? You don't have a job now, so we could just *go* there and maybe have a farm and—"

He held up his hand. "Ivy, me love. Ireland's a poor country, and there's no place in it for me anymore." His mouth drooped. "Nor here either, it seems."

This was so unlike him that she took fright. "No, don't!" she cried out.

"Ah, pay me no mind." He tousled her silky hair. "It's going to be fine, you'll see. It'll all work out just grand. Only a matter of time."

It had been months.

"Light a candle for me," he said, surprising her.

"Of course." She'd lit for him countless candles. She thought she could hardly bear it, she loved him so. "Maybe we could move to Staten Island?"

"Possibly. Or the moon."

"It's all so strange, isn't it, Pop? Getting born at all. And then living, and being yourself and not someone else. And dying in the end. Life is so *mysterious*."

"A great prince of your church, St. Augustine, when they beseeched him to explain the mystery of life and of time flowing, said, 'I know if you don't ask me.' "

Ivy frowned over the words. "It *sounds* like an answer. What does it mean?"

He smiled. "I know if you don't ask me."

TWENTY-TWO

Ivy AND HER FATHER were sitting in silence when
Francis and Megan came in with Pickwick, who made
for Megan's bed and flung himself down, panting.

"Isn't he young to get so tired from a walk?" Ivy
asked, wondering if there could be something wrong
with him. It would not do for him to get sick. In this
family, people had to stay healthy.

"He just doesn't like exercise," Megan said plac-
idly. "We met Frank, so we took a longer walk than
usual. And a cat looked at him. He's overexcited."
She gave her homely puppy a glance of total love
and understanding.

Looking at her brother and sister, Ivy thought that
there could not be, anywhere in the world, two more
gorgeous people. Cheeks glowing, hair tumbled from
the March wind, an aura of outdoor cold still sur-
rounding them. She didn't think that either Frank or
Megan gave a thought to their own looks, or to any-

one else's. Was that possible? It seemed to be. But *seem* was a tricky word.

"Where're we going this afternoon, Pop?" Frank asked. "I'll get the slips of paper."

"Not for me," said Ivy.

"Huh?" Frank and Megan stared at her. "What d'ya mean, not for you?"

"I just don't . . . today I think I'll go to the library. By myself."

"Yeah, but—" Frank turned to his father. "Can she do this?"

"I don't see why not. A person can't be held to a schedule of entertainment. If we make Saturday afternoon rambles a matter of obligation, the spirit would go out of them, surely."

"I still don't—" Frank began, then lifted his shoulders. "Okay. So it's you and me and Pop, Meggy. You want a slip of paper, or will you just go along with what I want?"

Anyone else, thought Ivy, would ask first what did he want. Not Megan. She smiled and said, "Sure, Frank."

"Then we'll go up to the park and skate. Okay, Pop?"

At Christmas, Aunty and Unk had given ice skates to the whole family, and they had, since then, gone several times to the rink up at Central Park. Even Mama had tried the ice twice, but couldn't get the hang of it and didn't want to. Pop, who'd learned to skate as a boy in Boston, was teaching the three of them, and they loved it.

For a moment, Ivy thought of changing her mind, but did not. Whenever she came really close to somebody else—either of her parents, once in a while Aunty, now and then Frank—Ivy felt a quickly following need to be by herself. It wasn't like that with Megan. She always felt close to her sister, no need to be out of her company. Being with her was sometimes actually like being alone, the way you'd be alone with a bunch of flowers or a little animal. Music, perhaps.

Now Pop looked at Ivy, nodded a couple of times to show he understood, and said to the other two, "Let's get cracking, then."

"Can we eat there?" Francis asked. "Hotdogs and hot chocolate, oh boy?"

Of late, they'd usually had sandwiches at home before setting off of a Saturday afternoon. It wasn't as much fun but of course was cheaper. Here and there, Mama and Pop were shaving expenses. Not where Holland was concerned. In other ways. No movies. Meat only once a week. At Christmas, except for the ice skates, they hadn't got things to play with. Shoes, and a book each. Even Aunt Anna had sent hand-knitted sweaters instead of the usual grab bag of puzzles and building sets and puppets and things that wound up— Of course, they were getting old for that sort of stuff.

But once . . . ah, once Aunt Anna had sent the most wonderful gift they'd ever had. An entire wooden farm, with a little house, a barn, trees and fences, a hay wagon piled with yellow wooden hay, farmyard animals from cows down to a tiny painted rooster. Even six little telephone poles with wires strung between them. They'd played with it for a couple of years. Then, in the move from Broadway to Inwood, it had somehow got lost. The worst loss they had ever known. Even now, long after she wouldn't be playing with it anymore, Ivy felt a sense of bereavement thinking of their lost toy farm.

When the others had taken the ice skates and set off, she sat in her father's Morris chair and moped for a while. They could have begged her, couldn't they?

Pickwick came into the room and sat looking at her, holding his right paw to his chest, as he had that first night when he'd been so lost and frightened and cold.

"What's the trouble now?" she asked in a pleasant voice, since Pickwick went to pieces at any hint of reproach. "You are not cold or frightened or lost anymore. You are probably the best-loved animal in Manhattan." She curled her right hand against her chest. "See how soppy it looks?"

Pickwick stood, advanced cautiously, and sat beside her, wagging his skinny tail.

"You," she said cheerfully, "are the dopiest dog I have ever seen. Why do you go on acting so sorry for yourself? You are *cherished*. What more do you want?"

He could very well ask me that, she said to herself. Pickwick wasn't the only creature in the parish flopping in a puddle of self-pity.

She went to the kitchen, closely followed, and fixed

herself a lunch of milk and saltines with peanut butter and jelly. After he'd drunk the milk she poured for him, Pickwick clicked back to the bedroom to wait.

I suppose, thought Ivy, he wouldn't actually bite any of the rest of us, but he sure wouldn't notice if we went out the door and never came in again.

She moved about restlessly. Go to the library? She wanted to, but it was so cold outside. Frigid. Glacial. She thought she was starting a cold. Her throat was sore. She shouldn't have gone with them skating even if she'd wanted to. Still, it was only five blocks to the library.

The trouble was—could she run the risk of really getting sick? Connie had said once that it must be swell, having a nurse for a mother, because then if anything happened, you'd have somebody around who knew what she was doing. "I love being sick," she'd said. "Not so I *hurt* or anything, or upchuck. What I like is having a nice temperature and staying in bed with books and games and ginger ale. And Daddy always brings me a present. He says invalids should get presents every day."

Ivy would not tell even Connie that the truth was her mother panicked when somebody in the family was sick or hurt. She didn't forget her nursing, and she always knew what to do, but she did it in a kind of rage.

"I *can't* get sick," she said aloud. "I will *not get sick*."

She took the mailbox key from a nail in the kitchen and walked out to the entrance between the court-

yard and the lobby, where the mailboxes were arranged in tiers. Even here, still indoors, the extreme
cold made her shiver. She put off thoughts of the library, grabbed the mail, and ran back to the warmth
of the apartment.

A few bills. A letter from Aunt Anna. Ivy patted the
envelope, glanced at the clock. Three-thirty. Unless
an emergency arose at the hospital, Mama would be
home soon. Her private-duty patient had gone home,
and the new one wasn't coming till the next day.
Which would give Mama a good night's sleep.

She sat in her father's Morris chair with *Jane Eyre*,
which she was rereading. She had fallen in love with
Mr. Rochester. Handsome, mysterious, passionate
Rochester, who loved plain Jane above all other
women. If I'd lived then, she told herself, I could have
been Jane. Short and plain and lonely. Also intelli-
gent and capable of passion. She knew she did not
understand yet what was involved in passion, except
through Jane's descriptions, but when the time came,
she'd know it, and she did not think it had anything
to do with having babies—a process that had been
carefully explained to them by their mother in simple, clinical terms that made it sound very unattractive. A married couple with children was one thing,
passion altogether another.

Had her father and mother, before they were married, before they had three children to interfere,
known that *other?* She pushed the thought away.

But one day . . . one day, when *she* was grown,
would she know what it was to have a man's arms

around her, a man's lips on hers, a man's *body* on hers? "No, no, no!" she said. That was the path to Father Cusick's confessional. She did not want to tell Father Cusick about these imaginings, so she'd better stop having them.

She closed the book, went to consult the kitchen clock, came back to the living room and moved about, fingering things. Nearly four o'clock, and where was her mother?

"Ivy, you are stupid," she said out loud. Extremely stupid, she added silently. There would never be a Rochester in her life. There had been only one Rochester. And he, she thought with a sudden thump into reality, had been only in Charlotte Brontë's lonely mind.

And her throat was really getting sore. She took two aspirin, examined her face in the medicine-chest mirror. Was she flushed? Getting something? If so, how could she keep it from Mama?

"What a pain in the neck everything is!" she said, as her mother came in the door.

"Talking to yourself, dearie?"

"Sometimes I do. There's a letter from Aunt Anna."

Mrs. Larkin waited until after dinner to open the letter, something Ivy would have been incapable of. To delay reading a rejection from Victor Ryland, ass't editor, was one thing. But a letter from Aunt Anna? How *could* she wait?

Mama said she liked to carry a letter around for a while first. She said she wanted to savor, not gobble.

"When your father was fighting in France," she told them, "I sometimes would carry one of his letters for a couple of days before I opened it. It *warmed* me."

"Suppose it had been bad news?" Frank had asked. "Suppose he was writing to tell you he'd fallen in love with a French mamzelle?"

Mrs. Larkin laughed. "Then I'd have been sure of his love that couple of days longer, wouldn't I?"

Tonight, when she finished the letter, she handed it to her husband. She did not look warmed.

"Well," he said, when he'd read it. "Nothing to do but tell them."

"Tell us what?" Ivy cried out, already in a panic.

"You can't go to the farm this year," Mrs. Larkin said flatly. "I'm sorry, but that's how it is. I'll read it to you. She says: 'Dear family, It is a sad thing to have to tell you, but I do it this early to keep the children from anticipating something that will not be possible, not this year. It makes me feel awful to say that we can't see how we can have them here this summer.'" Mrs. Larkin broke off, looked at their stricken faces, and sighed. "Well, let's see. She goes on: 'Tess is *quite* unwell, and we are having all kinds of trouble coping with her, and you know, Moira, that children upset her even more than she is usually upset, and now she is much worse. It's sad. I'm sorry about all of it, but all we can think to do now is try to keep her routine undisturbed. I know that you and Jack will understand and hope so much that the children will. We'll miss them very much.

" 'By the way, I should tell you that that bearskin you hate so much is gone. A hobo slept up in the loft one night and fell in love with it, so remembering how you feel about the thing, we gave it to him. You should have seen him waddling down the road with the bear's head on top of his and the rest dragging in the dust. I do hope nobody decides to shoot it again.

" 'The rest of us are well. I am so very, very sorry about the summer, but what can we do. Love.' "

Mrs. Larkin folded the letter and looked up in a helpless way. "You can see, can't you, children, that there *is* nothing else she can do. Poor Anna. And poor Tess. Tess has had such a—a meagre life. But I know what it means to the three of you, and all I can say is, I'm sorry."

"Ah, gee," said Frank. "It's—darnit anyway. I was going to drive the tractor by myself this year, Uncle Jim said. And go with him to a cattle auction. *Darn-it!*"

"Is Aunt Tess going to die?" Megan asked.

"No," Mrs. Larkin said sharply. "I mean," she went on in a gentler voice, "we certainly hope not."

I don't hope not, Ivy thought. If she did, maybe we could still go up there. Gone, gone . . . the real farm now as lost to her as the wooden toy farm. The hayloft empty of her sad brown bear. What does she mean, she knows what the farm means to us?

There was nothing left of all that was her own, had *been* her own. You exaggerate, she told herself, and answered I do not! Oh, no! Everything is gone. *Why* hadn't she walked to the library this afternoon and really gotten sick? Why hadn't she walked for miles in the freezing, damp day and got pneumonia that would make her die?

Next day, she didn't even have a sniffle.

TWENTY-THREE

ONE NIGHT THE FOLLOWING WEEK, Ivy wakened in the dark to a whimpering sound and wondered for a moment if another dog had nosed out Megan and was waiting in the courtyard to be rescued. Then there'd come a sharp cry, and she realized it was her brother she was hearing.

She crept around Megan's bed to his side and whispered, "Frank? Francis . . . are you having a nightmare?"

"Oh, God, I'm dying. I can't *stand* it anymore. I've been standing and standing it for hours, but I can't—"

Ivy rose. "I'll call Pop."

"No! Oh, golly. Oh, Jesus, Mary, and Joseph! I think I'm going to die—"

"What is wrong?" she said shrilly. "Where do you hurt?" Had his appendix burst? Was he having a heart attack? Could he have a heart attack at his age? "Frank, will you please tell me!"

"Toothache. My tooth's *killing* me."

"Oh. Well, that's not so bad."

Frank shuddered so that the bed shook. "You try having a— Oh, I'll just have to die. I can't take this anymore—"

"Shall I get you some aspirin?"

"What's the matter?" Megan said softly. "Frankie, are you hurting?"

"Oh, boy. Hurting. I'm just about crazy."

Megan put on the bed lamp, and the sisters watched their brother roll from side to side, the blanket clenched in his fists, knees tight to his chest. He was sweating and breathing in short gasps.

"I'm getting Mama," Ivy said.

"No!"

"I am. This is dumb. You can't just lie there and suffer. Mama will know what to do."

She would, of course. Pop said the reason she got so upset over illness in the family was that she knew entirely too much about all the terrible things that could happen to people. Polio. Scarlet fever. Tad Fregosi's brother, Ivan, had *died* of meningitis. He'd been only twelve years old, but he died just the same.

Besides, Pop said, Mama couldn't take time off from work to tend to sick children, and he couldn't either, and they couldn't bear the thought of leaving sick children at home all alone.

"It'd send anyone into a frenzy," Pop had said, and with a glance prevented her from making the obvious response that it did not send him into one.

"Some people are tougher than others," he said. "Your mother takes things very hard, with her worrying nature."

After her terrified reaction at being awakened in the night by one of the children, Mrs. Larkin took charge with her usual mixture of crossness and compassion. Gently touching Frank's jaw, she sent her husband to the bathroom to fetch aspirin and paregoric, Ivy to the kitchen to boil water for the hot-water bag, which was then wrapped in a towel and laid carefully against Frank's face.

Nurses did not sit on the patient's bed, so Mama knelt beside him, pulled the covers over his shoulders, studied him carefully, and said, "Now, you just have to put up with it, Francis. There's nothing to do until you see the dentist tomorrow, and he'll probably pull it. Fortunately, it's a back molar and won't show. It may even be a wisdom tooth. We might be lucky enough for that."

"Lucky!" Frank moaned. "I can't stand this until morning, Mama!"

"All the same, you will." Mrs. Larkin rose. "Back to bed, you two. Turn off the light, and don't keep him talking. He'll go to sleep with the paregoric. If he doesn't, call me."

In the dark Megan and Ivy lay obediently silent, but Frank, after a while, said in a muffled voice, "I wonder what animals do? They must get toothaches. How do they stand it?"

"Oh, my *goodness*," said Megan, at a new and clearly dreadful notion.

"That's great, Frank," said Ivy. "Just peachy, that was."

"I'm sorry." He groaned. "This hot-water bag is getting cold."

"I'll change it. Lie still and keep still. Try to let the paregoric get to you."

But when she returned from the kitchen, Megan was saying, "I don't see why an elephant's tooth should ache more than a mouse's. I think a mouse's toothache would be quite as bad for him as yours is bad for you, and *he* doesn't get paregoric."

"Elephant. Mouse. Me. Awful for all of us." Frank was beginning to sound drowsy. Ivy put the wrapped warm rubber bag next to his cheek and said, "Good night, Frank. Stop talking."

She turned out the light and got back in bed.

After a while, he did seem to doze, but went on moaning. Mama came in to look three more times, using her little nurse's flashlight. When it was scarcely light outside, she telephoned the dentist, waking him up with the information that her son had suffered more than enough and that her husband would be around to the office with the boy in fifteen minutes . . . all right, half an hour, but not a moment longer. It was not only her family that Mama could be strict with. Her son was in pain, and he was going to be seen to.

214

TWENTY-THREE

Mrs. LARKIN WAS SINGING AGAIN, a song Ivy had often heard before, about wishing she could shimmy like her sister Kate. Ivy didn't know what *shimmy* meant, and had never thought to ask, but it sounded *peculiar*. She watched as her mother ironed the second of her husband's two white shirts, the ones he wore job-hunting. Pressing the collar, the cuffs and a strip down each side of the buttons, she left the rest scored with wrinkles and hung it on a wire hanger.

Ivy, looking on, frowned. "Suppose he wants to take his jacket off?"

"If he lets me know in good time, I'll iron a whole one."

"What's shimmy mean?" Megan asked.

Mama wriggled her hips a little. "That."

"Does Aunty Kate shimmy?"

"Used to. She was pretty good at it. No more, of course."

"Why not?" Ivy asked.

215

"Well, honey. She's married."

"Does everything come to a stop when people get married?"

"Of course not. Some things do. You put aside childish things."

"Like what?"

"Oh, Ivy. Hopscotch."

"I put that aside ages ago, and I'm still not married."

"Double dates," Mrs. Larkin went on. "Love letters." She sounded wistful.

"I don't think I'll *get* married." No one will ask me.

Mama unrolled one of her starched and dampened uniforms and began on it, showing more care than she'd given her husband's shirts. "No wrinkled nurses on *our* floor," she said.

"I think marriage is sad and dull," Ivy persisted.

"Sorry we've given you that impression."

"Not just you. I think all married people are the same. Nothing interesting ever happens to them." When her mother did not reply she said, "I don't see how you can sing when Pop still hasn't got a job."

Mrs. Larkin tipped the iron up and looked intently into her elder daughter's eyes. "I have this streak of cheerfulness, Ivy, which I do my best to suppress, but it keeps rearing its silly head."

Ivy smiled. "Pop will find a job, won't he?"

"Of course." Mrs. Larkin finished one uniform, looked at the other, and tossed her hands up. "Let's have a pot of tea and some cookies."

At the table—Ivy and her mother with regular cups, Megan using a small china tea set sent to her at Christmas by Aunt Tess, who hadn't sent the rest of them anything—their mother said, "Just the same, it's certainly true that no matter how bad things seem, you can always find someone worse off."

Ivy thought of the old man turning over garbage. "I know that. Who's worse off, especially?"

"I was thinking of the Murphys."

Patch Murphy had crawled into the dumbwaiter in the basement of his building. His brothers, on the fifth floor, had tried to haul him up. They were not strong enough to hold the ropes, and Patch had plummeted three stories. He was in a Bellevue Hospital charity ward with both legs broken.

"Those boys are *always* up to something dangerous," Mama said, shaking her head. "I wonder would it do any good to forbid Frank to see them?"

Megan and Ivy said together, "No, it wouldn't."

"They're his friends," Megan said. "He'd be lonesome with no friends."

"Surely at the school he must have—" Mama began, broke off, and rushed to a diversion. "We should do something for the Murphys. Bake them a cake, maybe." Her daughters looked at her skeptically. "Well, we could visit Patch in the hospital. Take him a book."

She will not give us an opening to talk about the school, Ivy thought resignedly. She's so sure we'd criticize. We wouldn't, probably. Megan likes the place, and I don't care anymore. What you mean is, she told herself, you care so much that the only thing left is not to care. She was coming to know that people—animals, too—after a while endured a situation if there was no way out of it. She'd read that the more an animal in a spring trap strained to escape, the tighter the trap munched down. A fox would gnaw his paw off to get free, but most creatures gave up and waited to die of pain and starvation; or, with luck, be found in time by the trapper and killed.

She couldn't think what would be a parallel, in a human being, to a little fox gnawing his paw off, but knew that whatever kind of courage it would take, she didn't have it. Not to get out of The Holland School; not, like the fox, to save her life.

They went to see Patch in the hospital, taking him some of Aunty's cookies and a bag of balloons to blow up, because Francis said a book would make him even more depressed than he already was.

Spring came slinking into the city, tracking mud everywhere. Mr. Sudowsky, the butcher, and Mrs. Perine, the iceman's wife, ran away together, to the astonishment of the neighborhood. Nothing Mrs. Perine did would surprise them. But who, as Mr. Larkin put it, would've thought to cast Sudowsky in the role of the playboy of the Lower East Side? "Anyway," he said to his wife, "you can't put that into your category of 'who's worse off than ourselves.' Not where Perine is concerned. He seems cheerier than ever, and presumably the happy couple is happy?" Mrs. Larkin didn't answer.

"Well, there's plenty of people *better* off than us,"
Ivy said to her brother, who said tell him something
else new. Ivy tried, seriously, to recall when anything pleasant had been said, or had happened, in
her family.

Days were not so bad, with all of them busy. But
evenings were awful. Pop nearly unspeaking, the rest
of them nervously overcareful of each other's feelings, in case somebody's should get out of hand and
topple them into *outspoken* despair. The object of their
times together became to keep up a front. It didn't
persuade, but kept them at least polite. Could people
never know the good times unless bad times came
upon them? We used to notice or not notice each other
without noticing which we were doing, she thought,
longing for those times when they'd been free from
care and *had not known it.*

Ivy wished that every evening she could make her
mind quite blank, the way you'd take an eraser and
sweep a blackboard clean. But the mind paid no attention to what you asked of it, which was very peculiar, since it was with your mind you did the asking.

"Oh, *hell!*" she said out loud one night. Neither her
mother nor her father so much as glanced at her.

Then something lovely happened, but only to herself.

On the last Saturday in April, she walked to the
library, delighting in the mild air. It had been like
this for days, and signs of true spring, of the coming
summer, were everywhere. Stoop-sitters and win-

dow-leaners were to be seen after months of absence. Stickball had returned to the streets. The chant of the rag-dealers was heard again. *"I cash close!"* they cried in foghorn voices. *"I cash close!"* as they pushed their barrows of old apparel through the alleys. Street-cleaning trucks cruised slowly, throwing fans of water toward the gutters.

Coatless and content, Ivy went to return *Villette*, and there was Miss Lerner behind the desk.

Ivy stood for a moment, breathless, and then rushed forward. "You're back!" she shouted.

Miss Lerner smiled her perfectly beautiful smile. "I didn't let you know because I knew you'd be coming in, and I wanted it to be a surprise."

"Oh, it's a gorgeous surprise! The nicest surprise I—it's *marvelous!* But what about Brooklyn? You said it was closer to your home in—"

"I've moved back to Manhattan, and Mrs. Hargreaves wanted to go back uptown, so here I am."

Here she was!

"I loved your Christmas card. And your letter." She would not tell about keeping them in *The Harp-Weaver*. That did not seem a thing to tell even Miss Lerner.

"Well, I enjoyed yours very much." Miss Lerner reached for the book. "Ah. That's what I've always done, found one writer I loved and read the whole *oeuvre*."

"Oeuvre?"

The librarian smiled. "Fancy way of saying the

writer's works. In this case, three? Are you reading all the Brontës?"

Ivy nodded. "Anne's not the best, but I've done her—oeuvre, too. That's a nice word. I've got *Wuthering Heights* at home now."

Miss Lerner did not suggest that *Wuthering Heights* might be over her head, though in fact it was. Way over.

"My father's been out of a job for ages," Ivy blurted. This was the first person she had said it to. *Confessed* it to, as if it were a sin.

"Oh, Ivy. I am so sorry. What does he do?"

"He's an electrician with the— I mean, he used to be with the Board of Transportation. Now he just looks for work. All the time. It's awful. Everybody's so—nervous."

"Being out of work is frightening for the whole family."

"You're telling me."

"He'll find a job, Ivy. He's bound to."

"That's what we've been saying. Ever since November."

"Oh, dear. I wish there were something I could say to help you."

"You help. I like seeing you. You're going to stay?"

"So far as I know. Yes, I'll be here."

Ivy sighed, satisfied. She turned away, turned back. "Miss Lerner, do you think a person my age who's not even five feet tall might grow up to be a midget?"

"Now, Ivy, really."

"I have a seven-year-old sister practically my height. I feel like somebody standing in a hole all the time." She smiled nervously.

Miss Lerner stood, walked toward the stairs, carrying *Villette*. "Come on, we'll find you something a bit less—less strangling than *Wuthering Heights*. I think you need something lighter just now. Have you read *Green Mansions?*"

Ivy had, but she shook her head.

As they climbed the stairs, Miss Lerner said over her shoulder, "How tall am I, Ivy?"

They reached the second floor landing. "I don't know," Ivy said. "I never thought."

Miss Lerner slipped out of her high-heeled shoes and stood looking into Ivy's eyes. Miss Lerner had to lower her own eyes only slightly.

"Just over five feet. It used to trouble me, when I was a child, being short. But I stopped bothering about it when I got to college. You could stop bothering much sooner if you wished."

"I wish, all right," Ivy said wryly. "But I'm only four-feet-eleven."

"And—fourteen years old, right? You have some growing time," Miss Lerner said confidently. "Do you know why you never thought about me? How tall I am, that is?"

"Because I like you, I guess."

"Of course. You don't notice unimportant things about people you like. You notice *them*, whole beings, people you care for, whether they're five feet tall or seven feet tall in seven league boots."

"I'd notice that," Ivy said with a laugh. She was feeling really good. "I've read *Green Mansions*." She did not want, in any way, to be deceptive with Miss Lerner.

"Good. We'll think of something else. How about Irish plays? Have you read any of those?"

"No. My father loves them. He comes from Ireland."

"We'll try you on Yeats. Very poetic, and mystical and mysterious. Sad, sometimes. Not the mad sadness of Emily Brontë. An Irish sadness. Misty and musical. Would you like to try?"

Ivy nodded. She loved the way Miss Lerner talked. She loved everything about Miss Lerner, and she was happy. Happy!

They knew, the moment their father walked in on an evening in May, that it had happened. It was as if a light long extinguished had been relit.

"Jack!" Mrs. Larkin flew across the room into his arms. "You did it! You got one!"

He hugged her, and his children, and they were all laughing and asking questions at once. Indeed, he had got a job, and he'd better prepare them—

"Prepare us?" Mama said anxiously. "For *what*?"

Pop did a buck-and-wing. "You are looking, my darlings, at a sixty-dollar-a-week man! What better could I be saying than that atall?"

223

"I could use a raise," said Francis.

"Oh, my goodness," said Mrs. Larkin. "It's hard to take it in. Sixty dollars a *week*. How did you do it, Jack?"

"Application, mavourneen. Diligence. Perseverance. Oh, yes—and Vincent."

"Vincent?"

" 'Twas he got me the job. *Po*sition. One of the electricians at the *World-Telegram* suddenly got gathered to his fathers, and with my ability and a brother-in-law who was Johnny-on-the-spot, it's I who've stepped into his empty shoes."

"God rest him," said Mrs. Larkin and added, "Oh, what a piece of luck!"

They even laughed at that. Hurray for Unky, thought Ivy. Hurray for Pop! Hurray for all of us!

Mr. Larkin stretched and yawned, a man at the finish of a long and terrible race. "He came and got me and hustled me over to the personnel persona at the paper, the way I'd be the first to apply. Well, there's no saying how I feel. Vince will always be a Republican, but from this out, I'll not hear a word against the man. Listen—he and Kate are coming right over, and we are all going to Chinatown for dinner. Vincent's treat. A celebration."

"You accepted a *treat*?" Mama said, kissing him on both eyes and then his mouth. "What about your pride, sir, that you've been talking about all this while we've been eating stone soup?"

"Don't twit me, Moira me love. Not now, not on this day!"

224

They were seized with tumultuous joy. A job! Chinatown! Sixty dollars a week!

"Can Pickwick come with us?" Megan asked.

"If he sits quietly under the table, like the little gentleman we all know him to be, I think it will be all right. I feel that no one anywhere can refuse us anything this night," said their father, and he let out a yell of rapture.

Hours later, lying in bed, her brother and sister and Pickwick long asleep, Ivy brooded in the dark. No one anywhere can refuse us anything this night, Pop had said, and he'd been right. The people in the restaurant in Chinatown had smiled upon Megan and assured her that her puppy was welcome any time. Which had nothing to do with Pop's good fortune. Whoever refused Megan anything?

But if Pop felt no one could refuse him, no matter what he wanted this night, wasn't he equally bound not to refuse someone else her wish? He and Mama both? In their great good luck, their relief, their happiness, would they not agree to a thing that meant everything to their daughter?

Francis and Megan could continue to go to Holland. They liked it there, and the dear knew everybody liked them. Mr. McClellan, the Latin teacher, had written in Megan's autograph book, "Cynics say the world's askew. They should get a glimpse of you!" Megan wasn't in his class, was nowhere near ready for Latin. He'd written "Lots of luck" in Ivy's book.

She went on talking to herself, aware of outside

night sounds. Traffic passing, people going by in the courtyard, the bell of Father Cusick's church telling eleven o'clock.

I'll finish out the year, and she can't say then that I haven't given it a try, but even Mama must admit that some tries don't work out. Some people don't fit into some places, and that's life and she can't change what is because she wants it to be otherwise.

I will have given it a year. That's enough.

Pop will understand, surely. Why should I gnaw my foot off, when all they have to do is spring the trap and set me free?

I will go to the parochial school so Mama can have her way about no public school, which is dumb, but she's dumb sometimes and that's fine. Who isn't?

But!

But I am almost fifteen years old and not to be "led astray by nuns." I can think for myself. I'll just make them admit it. *I can think for myself.*

She got out of bed, while her courage was high, and went to tell her parents her decision.